If the killer was messing with their minds, he was doing a bang-up job.

The lobby area appeared clear. "I think we're—"

Gunfire exploded and sparks on the metal railing burst into the air. Cash's ears rung. Mae ducked and fired back. The killer must have been on the third-floor stairs, heard them moving and crept down.

Another shot fired. Mae winced and fired another round. Oh no.

"Mae, are you hit?" She was. She was in the crosshairs and hurt. Red seeped through her pale blue dress shirt. Cash threw open the door to the lobby and he and Mae burst through.

Going back in and giving chase was too dangerous. He wouldn't risk Mae's life and she'd already been hit.

"I'm okay." She breathed in sharply at the pain. "There's no way out of the building except on the first floor and there are a dozen exits at least."

"Split up." Mae wasn't a weakling. She was tough and capable, and while it terrified him letting her go alone, he trusted her to do the job she'd been trained to do.

Jessica R. Patch lives in the Mid-South, where she pens inspirational contemporary romance and romantic suspense novels. When she's not hunched over her laptop or going on adventurous trips with willing friends in the name of research, you can find her watching way too much Netflix with her family and collecting recipes for amazing dishes she'll probably never cook. To learn more about Jessica, please visit her at jessicarpatch.com.

Books by Jessica R. Patch

Love Inspired Suspense

Cold Case Investigators

Cold Case Takedown
Cold Case Double Cross

Fatal Reunion
Protective Duty
Concealed Identity
Final Verdict
Cold Case Christmas
Killer Exposure
Recovered Secrets

The Security Specialists

Deep Waters
Secret Service Setup
Dangerous Obsession

Visit the Author Profile page at Harlequin.com for more titles.

COLD CASE
DOUBLE CROSS

JESSICA R. PATCH

LOVE INSPIRED SUSPENSE
INSPIRATIONAL ROMANCE

LOVE INSPIRED® SUSPENSE

INSPIRATIONAL ROMANCE

ISBN-13: 978-1-335-55452-9

Recycling programs
for this product may
not exist in your area.

Cold Case Double Cross

For questions and comments about the quality of this book, please contact us
at CustomerService@Harlequin.com.

Love Inspired
22 Adelaide St. West, 40th Floor
Toronto, Ontario M5H 4E3, Canada
www.Harlequin.com

Printed in U.S.A.

Judge not, and ye shall not be judged:
condemn not, and ye shall not be condemned:
forgive, and ye shall be forgiven.
—*Luke* 6:37

For my soul sister, Heather. When God rebuilds, He builds stronger and with new stones. Our recent conversations brought Grandma Rose to life. PS: If you think you're going to hog Jesus when we make it to heaven, think again, friend!

There are so many people to thank for their help and support: my agent, Rachel Kent; my editor, Shana Asaro; my dear friends and brainstorming buddies Susan L. Tuttle and Jodie Bailey, excellent authors in their own right; my friend and ADA in my county Luke Williamson, for answering endless texts about the justice system and legalities; and to the retired rock star Desoto County CID detective (among a whole litany of titles you've achieved in your career) Jerry Owensby, who helped me tremendously with getting Cash Ryland and his job with the SO right! Any mistakes are my fault or stretched for the sake of the story.

ONE

Dread burst in Mae Vogel's gut, mimicking the intensity of the red, white and blue fireworks exploding over the lake on this Fourth of July night. She'd taken a week of vacation—but she had every intention of letting her unit chief know it shouldn't count. Since Mae stepped foot in her small hometown of Willow Banks three days ago, it had been nothing but stressful and tense, which was a far cry from vacation.

If Dad wasn't dogging her for choosing a "man's job" then he was ignoring her to pat her younger brother Barrett's back. Only two years her junior—and also in law enforcement—it had always been clear he was the favorite child. If Mae had been born with a y chromosome, maybe Dad would be proud that she was a cold case agent with the Mississippi Bureau of Investigation.

A small child crying caught her attention. "Hey, bud," she said to the preschool boy. "Did you lose your mom?"

His little, pitiful head nod broke her heart. The patriotic music medley against the backdrop of an enormous fireworks display was deafening. Willow Banks Park sat in darkness as families nestled on quilts to endure mosquitoes and ants while publicly celebrating freedom.

Children raced to beat the debilitating heat from devouring their patriotic popsicles. Food trucks, lemonade counters, and stands selling glow-in-the-dark bracelets, wands and necklaces abounded. But this boy had neither popsicle nor glowing beacon, and he wasn't the cause of her nervous energy coupled with apprehension. Something felt off, almost tangible. The night didn't feel free.

"I'm a police officer. I'll help you find your mom." He lifted his arms, trusting and afraid. Bless him. She scooped him up and he wrapped his sticky hands around her neck and laid his snotty nose against her shoulder. Her maternal gene kicked in, surprising her. Rarely did she let herself imagine being married or a mom. Some things simply weren't meant to be.

A woman came running through the crowd. "Parker! Oh," she cried and clutched her chest, a glowing bubble gun in one hand and cotton candy in the other. The little boy—clearly Parker—hollered and went to sobbing, reaching for his mother.

"Mommy!"

The frazzled woman thanked her. "I let go of his hand to pay for the cotton candy and he was just gone!"

"No problem. I was taking him to the security booth." Parker reached out again and his mother embraced him.

"You scared me to death, little man." She smiled and thanked Mae then disappeared into the night. One good deed done. Small towns could project a facade of safe living, but Mae had been in many of them working unsolved homicides with her team. Some of them child cases.

No place was truly safe.

But for a moment she was going to take her mind off

the job, the tension with her family and her grandma Rose's failing health, which was why she was on vacation here instead of somewhere tropical.

She moved toward the lawn chairs Mom and Grandma Rose were sitting in, glanced up at the radiant display and smacked into marble.

Nope. A man.

She peered up to apologize, but the words died on her lips as recognition dawned. Cash Ryland. Mae hadn't laid eyes on him, by design, since high school.

Maybe this was the origin surrounding her jittery feeling.

She put some pep in her step and moved backward, but Cash's tanned arm reached out, as if assuming she'd stumbled and not retreated from him.

She swatted away his steady hand. "I'm perfectly fine." No need for physical touch between them.

His thick eyebrows tweaked upward. "Sorry." His voice had grown deeper, huskier since he was a kid. Cash shoved his hand into his pocket, drawing her eye to the badge clipped to his thick black belt looping through well-fitted jeans.

What? How in the world did Cash Ryland make it into any branch of law enforcement and why would he want to? His teenage years had been spent as a juvenile delinquent. Not that she'd imagined what Cash might be doing now, but if she had it would be more along the lines of doing time for drug possession or grand larceny or maybe both. Not on the grounds with a criminal investigations division badge from Willow Banks Sheriff's Office.

Unbelievable.

"You never were too good at masking your feelings."

She glanced from his badge to his face and his lop-sided grin rolled another wave into her stomach. How dare her body betray her common sense by being attracted to his strong, chiseled features.

His blond hair had turned a little sandier, but it worked for him, unfortunately. His eyes hadn't changed—they were still the same intense shade of blue that won the hearts of girls determined to rebel against their parents. Cash had never been meet-the-parents material, unless a girl wanted to give them a heart attack and end up grounded for life.

Not Mae.

Mae knew better.

And she'd still been charmed then burned.

Speak, Mae. You have to at least speak. "I'm just surprised, I guess." As if she were still a high school girl enamored by the bad boy of Willow Banks and unsure of herself, she folded her arms, which felt like dead weight across her chest.

Cash Ryland—a detective. She'd seen it all.

"Well, it's a surprising thing. Um…" He scratched the back of his neck. "I actually was looking for you. I saw your family and hoped you would be here. Your brother mentioned you were in town on vacation."

Why did Barrett have vocal cords? He hadn't mentioned Cash to *her*. But then, why would he? Barrett was clueless about what had transpired during her senior year with Cash. All he knew was Mae had tutored Cash in English. But if anyone had been schooled that semester, it was Mae.

"Barrett talks too much." She tried to pass around him, but he blocked her. "Detective or not," Mae said, tossing grit into her tone, "if you don't move, I'm going to move you. And I promise you, size doesn't matter. I can do it."

While Cash towered above her five-foot-one frame, she was not porcelain, and attached to her petite frame was the muscle to maneuver him if necessary.

His hands shot up in surrender, but there was no teasing in his eyes. "I have no doubt, Mae. You've always been strong."

No one had ever uttered those words about her before, but flattery wasn't going to get him one solid inch. His charm no longer affected her.

He cleared a path for her to flee. "I just want to talk to you for a minute or two. Please?"

His voice and sharp blue eyes pulsed with desperation—a look and tone she'd witnessed dozens of times in family members who needed hope to cling to after a loved one's case went cold. It never failed to reach out and draw her compassion. Even now it hit her chest with a dull ache and rippled through her rib cage. His scruffy jaw and wildly handsome looks didn't hurt either. Ugh—she was a pitiful!

Reluctantly, she nodded. "Okay. Two minutes tops." So much for the tough agent persona she'd worked hard to depict. But desperation wasn't an emotion that could be easily faked. The loud music and fireworks in addition to shouts of joy and applause made hearing nearly impossible. Cash pointed to a more secluded area and she followed his long and purposeful stride. His broad shoulders squared—not in arrogance but in confidence and with a touch of swagger from the old days.

He'd always had sun-kissed skin, like his mother, who Mae had only briefly met once.

Cash leaned against a vending machine near the rest-rooms.

"Two minutes," Mae reminded him.

He nodded and held up his index finger. "First, I should have said it years ago, but I'm sorry for what I did. For what I took from you." His Adam's apple bobbed and his jaw worked as if fighting for composure. "I haven't been that guy in a long time, Mae. And, I've thought about you a lot over the years and how things ended."

Was he serious right now? Mae tossed him a humorous laugh. "How it ended? It *ended* with you stealing my English essay and handing it in as your own, leaving me with nothing to turn in." No one had even believed her, which was startling since Cash had never done any work that scholarly once in his life. But that was how things had always gone down for Mae. It was his word against hers and Mae had drawn the short stick. Cash barely passed the class using her paper and she lost out on 75 percent of the class grade. "It cost me the vale-dictorian spot. You catfished me and I fell hook, line and sinker. And now you want to ask me something by prefacing it with a weak apology. Like that's going to get you what you want. I beg to differ at your statement that you're no longer the same guy you used to be."

Her words hit their target. His face faltered with a pained expression, and resignation surfaced with a slow nod, as if he'd expected the swift rebuke. Cash was not stupid—even if he had referred to himself during tutoring as a lunkhead or a moron. She'd always redirected his negative self-talk and never believed it.

But he was all about taking the easy way out and shortcuts, hence the stolen paper.

"You're wrong, but I can see your point." And now he was going to argue with her. She bit back a remark.

"What do you want, Cash?"

"It's about my brother, Troy. You probably know he's been in prison for about fourteen months for murdering his ex-wife, Lisa."

Mae raised an eyebrow. What could she do for his younger brother? She'd only met him once or twice. "Barrett might have mentioned it. I can't say I remember. What about it?"

He gripped the nape of his neck and squeezed. "Troy's a lot of things—I'll be the first to admit it. But he's not a murderer, which means whoever did kill Lisa is roaming free. That makes her case a cold one."

Ah, now he was getting to his agenda. Help on a cold case.

"I've exhausted my resources. I'm only one man, and I've never claimed to be the sharpest tool in the shed."

"You're a detective, Cash. You're clearly bright enough to solve cases or you cheated on the exam." Sadly, she believed the former. Cash was sharp and smart even if she didn't like him and held a grudge about the past.

He shrugged off her subtle compliment—well, more fact than compliment.

"My point is that I've done everything from investigating to hiring a private investigator. I was wondering if you and your team may be able to look into it."

Before she could decline, he raked his hands through his hair. "It's killing me, Mae. Troy isn't doing well and the last few times we've talked he's mentioned ending it all. You're our last chance and if anyone is smart enough to get to the truth, it's you."

Mae pinched the bridge of her nose as "God Bless America" blared through the speakers. She couldn't help him and if she were being honest, didn't want to. "How concrete was the evidence that convicted him?"

"Overwhelming, but I'm telling you there's a whole lot that doesn't make sense. If you'll let me, I can show you the case files or share them with you by memory. I know every single word."

"You memorized case files?"

"I did."

Wow. Okay. But still. "If the evidence is overwhelming and you nor a PI could find anything new, then it sounds like it's not a cold case, Cash. It's a closed case. I'm sure you don't want to believe that your own kin could do something like murder an ex-wife, but it's possible that you can't find anything because there's nothing to find because he did it. Prison is hard on even guilty people. I don't see how I can help you."

Cash rubbed his temples. "I'm telling you he didn't do it."

"You also told me you didn't take my essay. But you did. And it appears—based on evidence and probably testimony—that your brother took a life even if says he didn't." Mae didn't try to soften the harsh blow. Cash needed to hear the truth in all its ugliness even if the disappointment and fear in his eyes unsettled her.

"I—I deserve that," he said quietly, looking away into nothing.

For a split second, Mae felt sorry for him. But that sweet tone and gorgeous face had messed with her head and her heart once before; it wasn't happening again. Detective or not, Cash Ryland couldn't be trusted. "Sorry, but I can't help you."

"No, I get it." He worked his jaw and let a defeated sigh escape his lips. "Apology still stands. I wish you well, Mae." He turned and slunk in the darkness, his shoulders no longer confident but slumped.

The decent human being inside her nudged her to catch up and offer a quick scan of the case files with no guarantees, even if the hurt high school girl with a broken and betrayed heart protested. One look wouldn't kill her. If anything, it would confirm she was right—closed case, not cold case.

She mentally kicked herself then chased after Cash, not completely sure where he'd gotten to. As she pushed through the crowd toward the woods on the edge of the park, she spotted him as he withered to the ground.

A dark figure bolted from behind Cash and tore through the congregated picnickers toward the trees.

Mae's heart lurched into her throat as she bolted to Cash then dropped beside him. His faced was pinched in pain and his hand was covered in blood.

"Cash!" she hollered over fireworks exploding in rapid succession as the climactic moment began to wind down the grand show. "Were you shot?"

"I don't know." Shock radiated in his voice. Mae lifted his shirt to inspect the wound and cringed. "You've been stabbed. Call it in, Cash. And keep pressure on the wound." She couldn't be sure of the damage due to the dark night and the amount of blood.

He clutched the radio from his belt. "Delta 3 SO, send me a car to the west side of Willow Banks Lake near the pavilion, and start an ambulance to this location. I have been stabbed but am stable. Repeat, I am stable."

Several first responders on duty ran in their direction, having heard Cash's call into the sheriff's office. And barely near the tree line, she spotted a dark figure. "You'll be okay, now." She jumped up and pursued the perpetrator. Weaving through families entranced by the fireworks overhead and oblivious to the fact that a detective had been stabbed, Mae rushed but lost the attacker in the shadows.

She kicked the grass and punched her palm. Heart racing, she doubled back to the scene. Ambulance lights flickered and Cash was being loaded onto a stretcher. "Cash!"

"Miss, you need to stand back," a first responder said.

Mae frowned and retrieved her badge and shoved it at the deputy. "Agent Mae Vogel, MBI. I witnessed the stabbing, so I think I'll be coming a little closer." Ignoring the deputy's scowl, she hurried to Cash. His eyes were closed and his face was pale; he wasn't as stable as he had let on and her stomach roiled. She flashed her creds and demanded information from the EMTs.

"He's lost a lot of blood," one of the paramedics said. "We need to move. Now."

"I'm coming with him." Mae didn't wait for permission and hauled herself into the back of the ambulance. It made sense to go along—professionally—since he was the victim and she was a witness who would need to give deputies a statement.

This had nothing to do with the fact that she'd once fallen hard for him.

Cash winced as the ER doctor finished stitching him up. He'd skated by on the skin of his teeth according to the doc. The stabber had been sloppy or in a hurry and missed Cash's major organs, but the deep wound hurt and the stitches hadn't helped. His entire left side burned and throbbed.

"I'm gonna give you a couple pain meds to hold you over until you can get a prescription filled tomorrow. Take them, Detective. You'll regret it if you don't." The doc handed him the script and pills and patted his shoulder. "And watch your back."

"Ah, funny. Stick to healing instead of humor," Cash teased and returned the shoulder pat. "'Preciate it." He squinted at the prescription with jumbled letters. Doctors' handwriting were rotten to begin with but it wouldn't have mattered if the letters were perfectly spelled out. Cash would have trouble reading them regardless.

He had dyslexia.

He hadn't realized it until his mentor and boss figured it out when Cash was eighteen and graduated high school. Until then, he'd figured what everyone else said about him was true—he was nothing but a below-average kid who could barely read or write.

Sometimes he still struggled with spoken words more than written ones. But at least he now knew there was more to his disability than simply not "getting it"—and knowing was half the battle.

Since the diagnosis, Cash had been figuring out how to navigate the world with his challenges. God had been faithful and placed the right people in his path at the right time to help him, whether it was going to the police academy or taking the test to make detective. But his dyslexia wasn't something Cash freely discussed.

At the moment, he was more concerned with how to

help Troy. Without Mae, Cash was lost, but he owed his brother. Cash was responsible for Troy's downward spiral into criminal activity because he'd been the one to introduce his brother to it when Troy was only twelve and Cash had been sixteen and mad at the world. Troy's misdemeanors hadn't helped him during his murder trial, and that Troy had physically abused Lisa had been the nail in the coffin.

Cash was convinced Troy didn't kill her, and whoever had was now targeting Cash.

It was no secret he never gave up investigating and he'd even been pretty vocal in bringing Mae—a cold case investigator—into the case. Anyone could have heard through the grapevine or firsthand, which meant the killer was in Willow Banks and most likely a citizen.

But Mae had turned him down and her bias against him fueled her negative response. Cash couldn't drop the ball now, though. Troy might not make it much longer and even though he'd been to a few church services in prison, he hadn't given his life to Jesus. The eternal consequences were too great and time was too short and not on either of their sides.

He exited the sterile, bleach-scented examining room and strode down the hall, the stitches pulling at his hot, fevered skin around the wound. Some of his colleagues had come in with him and taken a statement, rallied to support him and assure him they were after who hurt one of their own. But it had been a blitz attack and Cash had nothing concrete to offer. Mae might have seen more but he'd noticed that she hadn't been in the room. It would have lit up if she had. Mae was different from any other girl he'd ever known and her bravery and strength tonight proved she hadn't changed.

Memories invaded his mind as he followed the corridor to the lobby. Asking Mae for tutoring had seriously wounded his pride, but he'd desperately wanted to graduate high school and Mae had been the smartest—and kindest—girl he'd ever met.

He'd gone with the intent to charm her with his flirtatious ways and persuade her to tutor him. He was ashamed to admit he'd been pretty good with girls back then but the moment he'd entered Mae's personal space all his swagger and false bravado had disappeared and a shyness he'd never experienced had bubbled to the surface. No other girl had ever produced the buckled-knees effect on him or made him feel vulnerable and nervous.

Then he'd gone and betrayed her—one of his biggest regrets other than his bad influence on Troy.

As he rounded the corner, he touched his hand as if he could feel her holding it on the way to the hospital, but she hadn't been in the ambulance. Must be some weird dream he had when he passed out. He approached the lobby and did a double take.

Mae perched on the edge of a blue waiting room chair, bobbing her knee and resting her thumbnail against her two bottom teeth.

A couple of his colleagues remained and as Cash entered the waiting area near the lobby desk, they stood at attention and offered condolences and inappropriate jokes, lightening the heavy moment.

Cash appreciated their presence but all he wanted was to talk to Mae, who was gazing at him.

Surely, she'd already given her statement and could have left by now. *Had* she been in the ambulance with him?

Finally she stood and her expression teetered on con-

cerned. Mae Vogel concerned about him? He didn't deserve that but he'd take it.

"Are you okay?" She cautiously approached him,
looking at his wounded side.

"Sore as all get-out and I have some stitches, but I'll
live." He shrugged.

She met his gaze with sincerity and worry. Maybe
she didn't hate him as much as it appeared at the celebration. If looks could kill, he'd have already been
dead. But that wasn't her expression at the moment.
"I'm sorry I didn't catch him," she said. "He all but
vanished into the woods." She motioned with her head
to the few remaining colleagues. "I gave the detectives
my statement."

Two deputies and one of his CID colleagues grinned
from behind her, gave him thumbs-ups and waggled
eyebrows. Clearly, their deputy work was shoddy.
There was nothing romantic between him and Mae.
She stepped aside and he talked a few moments with
them and one by one they trickled out the glass sliding
doors, leaving only him and Mae.

"Hey, no worries you didn't catch him." The fact that
she'd sprinted off after the perpetrator alone was pretty
cool. It was her job—but it was well…kinda hot. Oh, he
could not be thinking along those lines. *Reel it in, Ryland. Reel. It. In.* Think case. "This proves I'm right."

She frowned. "How's that?"

"The real killer doesn't want me to investigate and
tried to shut me up permanently." Now Cash had even
more incentive to press forward.

"Is that what you told Detective Nicholson? He's the
one who took my statement, but I didn't see much. A

dark figure. As far as I know, no weapon was located at or near the scene."

"Shane. Yeah, I did." Cash refrained from admitting that Shane wasn't so sure Cash could or should be making those leaps, but he felt it in his bones. "It's too coincidental with the timing of the attack. And because they don't want me investigating, it tells me that out there somewhere is evidence against them."

Mae tucked a small strand of pale blond hair behind her ear. She wore it shorter now than in high school; it hung straight and thick to her collarbone but it was every bit as shiny and every bit a distraction. "Have you considered the possibility that your past is catching up to you and your attacker is an enemy with a score to settle?"

The question was legit but it stung regardless. Cash had done a lot of people dirty, cut corners while looking out for number one, but his life turned around at eighteen when he'd been caught dead to rights shoplifting. Since then he'd worked tirelessly to redeem himself by building an honest reputation that hung on integrity and faith. He'd also spent hours giving back to the community through outreach programs for troubled teenage boys.

He stroked his chin, thinking about that possibility. "You make a valid point, Mae, but it's been fourteen years since I got into any trouble. If you'd take a look at the case files, you'll see many things overlooked or not brought up by my brother's defense attorney or appealed by him. Troy was framed. I'm not biased. As much as I love my brother, if he were guilty I would expect justice to be served and his punishment to be exacted."

Mae held his gaze and pursed her lips then sighed. "Fine, Cash. I'll take a look at the case files—"

"They're at my house."

Mae raised her eyebrows. "Did you get special circumstances to do that?"

Taking home case files was frowned upon but not necessarily a hard rule.

"No, I don't have *special* circumstances." Not in the sense she was alluding to anyway, but he did have them due to his dyslexia, which meant he would need extra time to pore over them. But that was none of her business.

"Once a rule bender, always a rule bender." Her tone was cutting, which he expected. The only Cash she knew was the rule breaker and thief.

"One hour. That's all I'm asking for." A sharp twinge nailed the area around his stitches. He winced and clutched his side. "I'm not playing the pain card, but whether or not you come with me, I need to get home and take some meds."

She glanced at his side, the script in his hand and the sample of pain meds then sighed. "One hour. But, Cash, if I agree with the investigating officers, then that's that."

"Deal." He held out his hand and she hesitated then shook. Her hand was delicate but firm. Mae could no longer be defined as the prettiest girl he'd ever laid eyes on. She was a far cry from a girl, but she'd grown into the most striking woman he'd ever seen. And he wouldn't take for granted her sliver of mercy, which only added to her appeal. "This means so much to me, Mae. Thank you."

She raised her eyebrows in clear disagreement. "Don't thank me yet." She rubbed her hands on the sides of her shorts and sighed. "I'm gonna need a ride," she said as she walked outside with him. The sticky heat smacked him like a wet, hot towel and the smell of cigarette smoke assaulted his senses.

"I came by ambulance, in case you forgot." His joke produced an amused smirk from Mae. "I'll radio us a ride to the park to pick up our cars."

"No," she said in a curt tone. "I can call my brother." She pulled her phone from a denim fanny pack resting on her slender hip and in a few swipes had Barrett on the line. Cash didn't dislike Barrett but he had more attitude pumping through his veins than warranted.

"Hey, Barrett. You busy? I'm at the hospital…No I'm fine. I'm with Detective Ryland. He was…Yes, he's fine. But we need a ride to the park to pick up his un-marked unit and my car. I rode in the ambulance. We're out front of the ER…Okay, see you in five."

Apparently, Mae had picked up on the looks from the deputies and wanted to keep the rumors at a dis-creet minimum. He respected that she wanted things to remain professional.

"Barrett heard about the stabbing," she said and lifted her hair from her neck. Even this late, the humidity was merciless. "They've been combing the woods for evidence." She poked out her bottom lip and puffed air onto her brow. "How's he doing? On the job?"

Cash grinned and gave her a knowing look. "He's young and cocky."

Mae snorted. "He'll always be one of those two things. Comes by it honest."

He feigned shock. "You? Cocky?"

"Ha. Ha." She returned his teasing remark with a put-out expression. "My dad. When I went to the police academy, I got the riot act. When Barrett joined? Oh, he was the glorified hero."

In Cash's home, no one was the favorite. His folks had barely noticed two boys lived under the same roof as them. "Maybe your dad worries about you. Double standard, for sure. But I hear there's something special about a baby girl." He shrugged. What did he know of kids other than one day—if he had the option—he'd like to have a few? But it wasn't an option for him, which made committing to a woman pretty much impossible.

Most women wanted children. Unfortunately, passing dyslexia to a child—and it was a 40 to 60 percent chance—wasn't anything Cash would ever do. Willingly putting a child through the same torment he had endured was cruel and unfair. Some mornings he still woke up to those jokes and labels that had been hurled at him in class, halls and cafeterias.

Harsh words were like pieces of DNA. They formed a person. He didn't like the teenager he'd become and if he were honest, he didn't always like the man he was now.

Nope. He couldn't do it. Wouldn't do it.

"Cash, you hurtin'?" she asked.

"What? Oh. No. I'm fine."

Barrett pulled up in his marked unit and rolled down the window. "How you feelin', man?"

"Like I got stabbed." He grinned and ignored the burning pain.

"Imagine that," Barrett retorted as he hopped out of

the unit and opened the back door. Cash hesitated. It had been eons since he'd been in the back of a squad car and the memories left a sour taste in his mouth, but he stepped forward anyway.

"Dude, Mae can ride in the back seat." He frowned as if it was standard procedure. "Get up front."

Mae rolled her eyes.

"Barrett, ladies don't belong in back seats." He eased into the plastic seat and grimaced but refrained from groaning at the searing sensation.

Mae paused and caught his eye. Confusion drew a line across her brow, but she rounded the hood and climbed into the front seat. Barrett closed Cash's door and frowned then got in behind the wheel.

"You bought the Rigginses' old place when they moved, right?" Barrett asked.

Cash nodded and shifted to find a comfortable position.

"You fix it up?"

"Workin' on it." Cash loved the patch of land and little farmhouse. Open air. Room to breathe. It wasn't anything to write home about but he was remodeling it himself as time allowed. Which wasn't much between work, volunteering at the center for troubled teens and the mission trips he took on his vacation. He loved working with his hands and had a knack for carpentry and building. He'd helped construct more than eight churches in the last decade and he was proud of the work.

"Mom wondered what happened to you earlier," Barrett said to Mae. "I'll pass on informing her that you were chasing down a dude with a knife. She'll have a spell. What were you thinking?"

Mae leaned against the door, her head resting on the window as she stared into the night, ignoring Barrett. Seemed about all they shared were their blond hair, blue eyes and dimples.

Cash felt a bubbling need to stand up for Mae. "She was doing her job. Do y'all not know she's an agent with the MBI?"

Mae turned and caught his eye. He wasn't sure if she was thanking him or confused or both but she tossed him the saddest smile he'd ever witnessed and it punched his heart with more force than a hurricane. He returned it with a nod and she went back to resting her head on the window.

Barrett's response was a grunt then silence the rest of the way to the parking lot. He parked next to Mae's car first. "You coming home tonight?"

She cocked her head and sneered. "Well, yes."

Cash didn't appreciate the innuendo any more than Mae had.

A smug smirk played at Barrett's lips. "Okay, put the gun down, Maebelle."

She huffed and turned to Cash. "I know where the Riggins place was. Meet you there." Once she was in her car, Barrett drove to Cash's unmarked unit.

"If she doesn't make it home tonight, be discreet," Barrett warned.

"She'll make it home fine. She's helping me on Troy's case. Possibly reopening it."

Barrett grunted again and opened the back door for Cash, who carefully exited and thanked Barrett for the ride. Mae's headlights shone in his eyes but it cast enough light for him to see a problem.

He groaned and flagged her down with his right arm. She pulled over. "What's wrong?"

"Someone slashed my tires."

TWO

Cash yawned as Mae turned into his driveway, his body exhausted but his mind racing. An hour until midnight, but time wasn't on their side and sleep would have to wait.

Why had his tires been slashed? Cash couldn't see what purpose it would serve unless the jerk was simply testing out the knife on rubber before flesh. He tossed that sarcastic thought aside. In all likelihood it had been nothing short of rage—rage at Cash pursuing the investigation or rage that Cash had lived and not died out there at the park.

"Welcome to my house," he said as Mae pressed the engine button and turned off her car.

"It's nice." She woodenly exited the vehicle, her hands clutching her fanny pack. Even at this time of night, the humidity was suffocating and sticky. Crickets and frogs were in a contest to see who was the loudest. Cash liked the chirps and croaks, but under tonight's full moon, the sounds were ominous. "It's not what I was expecting."

"Were you expecting a meth trailer with a sagging roof and the smell of burnt plastic and acetone?" It wouldn't have been too far off base had his life not drastically changed thanks to his mentor Charlie Child.

Mae's eyebrows flinched. "I envisioned a bachelor pad. Certainly not flower beds out front and ferns hanging across the porch. You have a girlfriend?"

If he didn't know Mae and her up-front feelings for him, he might have taken that as a subtle inquiry into his eligibility. But he wasn't naive. She was here because of her compassion and because he had been nearly killed earlier.

"A guy can't like landscaping?"

Her smile was genuine. "I guess that was a little sexist, huh?"

Cash held up his index and thumb, revealing a tiny space between the two. "Just a little." He scanned his place. "I bought it to fix up on my own time. I like working with my hands. And out back is a large pond. I also enjoy fishing. It's carctic."

She frowned. "It's what?"

His stomach squeezed. "Uh…relaxing." He'd messed up words again. It happened occasionally but was more intense if he was nervous or exhausted—and right now he was both.

"Oh." She half smiled. "Cathartic."

"Yeah." He slapped his forehead as his neck and cheeks heated. "It's late and I'm tired." *And I'm dyslexic, so my words get jacked sometimes.* Why not come clean? He was a grown man, not that insecure little boy who'd been teased and picked on for being unable to read even the simplest of words. *Hey, the reason I stole that essay was there was no way I was going to graduate high school on my own. I was desperate. I'm sorry.*

But the words got hung on the shame—of what he

did and his condition. Girls' giggles and boys' taunts echoed over the truth. The hurtful words replayed on a loop. Even now he could feel that burning ball of nerves in his gut as he was forced to read aloud in Mrs. Kinley's third grade class, her eyes holding pity as he struggled and spectators snickered.

He hated pity.

He'd rather be a guy who did a rotten thing as a teenager before growing up into a responsible adult than have Mae look on him with the same pity. No need to feel sorry for him.

Locking down the memories and unlocking the front door, Cash entered his house and switched on a lamp nearby then dropped his keys into the dish next to it. "Come on in." He motioned Mae inside. It wasn't much but it was home.

She wandered into the living room, inspecting her surroundings. She paused at the entertainment center. "Was this here when you moved in?" She ran her hands along it with appreciation. "Handcrafted. I love it."

Cash's heart missed a beat and pride in his accomplishment ballooned in his chest. "I built that into the wall about six months after I got here."

She turned and her eyes were wide with wonder. "Wow. I'm impressed."

And that's how he'd like to keep it. Eyes of wonder and not pity. "Make yourself at home. You want coffee or lemonade…sweet tea?"

Glancing at his side, she grimaced. "Why don't you have a seat and I can find my way around to make coffee, if you don't mind."

Did he? No. Not at all. He eased onto the worn, brown leather sofa. "Coffee canister is beside the coffeepot, and the cups are in the cabinet above. I really appreciate it, Mae."

She gave a curt nod and scurried into the kitchen. The light flipped on and the whoosh of running water and clanking soothed him. It was nice having a woman in the kitchen—not the waiting on him but the sharing of space. He wouldn't get used to it, though. Leaning his head back on the sofa, Cash closed his eyes. He needed to take the meds, but they'd knock him out and he needed his faculties to go over the case with Mae.

The coffeepot gurgled. Rich brew wafted in the air and the air-conditioning kicked on with a low hum.

"About this case," she said as entered the living room, "or we can do it tomorrow. You look tuckered out."

"No, I'm fine." He forced himself into an upright position. "The paper files are beside the couch or I have scanned copies on my laptop. Which do you prefer? I like to look at the actual photos, which are included. Evidence is not." He started to stand, but Mae thrust a hand out to keep him parked.

"Paper." She hefted the cardboard box onto the coffee table, which he'd also built, and removed the lid. "Tell me about Troy."

To know Troy, she'd have to understand their upbringing—not that it was any excuse for the choices they'd made, but background never hurt. "Dad drank a lot—he passed two years ago from cirrhosis. Mom worked three jobs to keep food on the table and the small amount of clothing we had on our backs, so she wasn't home often or involved. I looked out for Troy and I can't say I was a model brother."

"I'm sorry," Mae said. "That must have been tough."

"It was our life. We didn't know anything else."

Mae flipped through the case file and her mouth slid into a hard line. "I see four calls in more than a year for domestic violence. Troy physically abused Lisa?"

Cash rubbed his dry, itchy eyes. "Troy drank too much. And when he did, it could turn ugly." Lisa had called Cash a few times before and he'd gone over there to deal with it, which sometimes included Cash physically restraining his brother. He'd begged Lisa to leave until Troy could get some help—maybe forever—but she never would. "I wanted Troy to get help before he sparrowed down Dad's road."

Mae flashed him a puzzled look. "Before he what?"

"Ended up like Dad."

"Ah. Spiraled. You are tired. You sure you don't want to do this tomorrow at the sheriff's office when you can think and speak clearly?"

Tired or not, it wouldn't matter if he was at the SO or not. He gritted his teeth as his ears fevered. "No. Look I know his behavior isn't exactly making him appear innocent. Troy made horrific choices. Those are on him." Not their father and not on Cash. But he did feel some guilt and responsibility being his brother. "Regardless, he didn't commit murder."

Mae's hardened expression hinted that she disagreed. "She was found beaten to death with Troy's baseball bat in her living room and his hair was recovered from her body along with some skin under her nails. When they arrested him, he had scratches on his hands." She held up a photograph. "I call this a slam dunk."

Cash could get with that. However. "He worked construction. The cuts could easily be consistent with working with tools, wood and machinery. Someone could have stolen his bat."

"A jury didn't seem to think so." The case was sinking. She was going to deny reopening it. "Not to mention, this says they had an argument at a bar the night of the murder."

He was aware. Cash had memorized the file with some help from Teri—a deputy and a church friend who knew of the dyslexia and had been given permission by Sheriff Powell to help Cash with reports and other things.

But he'd brought Troy's file home to study the photos again and see if there was anything at all he might have missed. The scans weren't as good of quality.

"True. They argued, but nothing turned physical. They were talking about getting back together."

"After the divorce?"

"Yes. They'd been divorced about six months. I know this is true because I saw Lisa's car a few times at Troy's. He told me he was going to get some counseling and work things out with her. But I never was called to the stand by the defense attorney to testify of this, which is strange all in itself."

"I'll give you that." She tapped her index finger on her chin as she continued to read the file. "He left the bar at 11:00 p.m. Bartender said he was sloshed and called an Uber driver to take him home. Troy states that he passed out in the car and the driver must have gotten him inside and put him on the couch. Who does that?"

"It's Willow Banks, Mae. Just about anybody would."

"He woke up with bloody hands and clothes. But he didn't call the police," Mae said as she held up the report, skepticism radiating in her blue eyes. "He showered and threw away his clothing, which was found in his trash can by the garage. Innocent people don't do that, Cash. You're a detective. What would you think?"

That the ex-husband had offed his former wife. "I know it looks sketchy."

"Troy easily could have pretended to be drunker than he was so that the bartender would call an Uber then faked passing out so the driver would testify the guy was sloppy drunk. After the driver left, he had time to drive the fourteen miles to his old home with Lisa and murder her. He has no alibi after the driver left the house. And the bloody bat was found in his shed."

All true.

"There's nothing concrete for me to take back to my unit chief. He'll side with me."

Cash raked his hands through his hair, desperation jackhammering under his skin. "I know it seems impossible, Mae. But look at tonight. Someone wants me to shut up. How do you explain that?"

The coffeepot beeped and Mae pivoted toward the kitchen. "How do you take your coffee?"

"A splash of cream is all, but I can get it." He hobbled in behind her but she was already pouring a cup in a yellow mug with a happy face. Cash retrieved the cream. "I have milk if you don't want the full stuff."

Mae held up her cup. "I drink it black. It's good."

"I got it from a roaster in New Albany."

After a few more sips in silence, Mae placed her mug on the counter. "I get wanting to believe the best out of the people you love. But family can disappoint us in ways we never imagined."

"Believe me, Mae, I know this." He'd been on both ends of that seesaw.

"You're a smart guy. A gut feeling isn't enough to

reopen a case, and nothing about your stabbing leads me—or anyone else—to believe that it's in connection to Troy's case. My hands are tied."

He'd feared she'd come to that conclusion. "Troy only had three beers. I've seen him put down an entire twelve pack and be lucid. Three beers wouldn't make him black out—as he puts it. He didn't fake being drunker or he'd have ordered more alcohol. He claimed he hadn't been drunk at all and someone slipped him a Mickey."

Mae huffed and carried her coffee into the living room. She took another sip, placed the mug on a coaster and grabbed the file, thumbing to the last page she'd been reading. "He admits to blacking out, at times, when drinking. He admits to waking up in strange places. But if he blacked out and claims he wasn't drunk, then it could have been a homicidal trance."

"You believe that?"

"You don't? Ever watched a video of a murder? I have and it's like they get tunnel vison and are only focused on their victim. I've seen a video of a person coming down the stairs and standing next to a man stabbing his victim and the guy never even knew the witness had been there. Troy said he couldn't remember. Often criminals will say they don't remember what happened—and this theory would prove why. Maybe Troy can't remember. Because he was in a homicidal trance."

Maybe. But it wouldn't stand up in court without scientific proof and a psychological professional who would testify to it. "Regardless, Mae. He only had three beers. He wasn't drunk. And he wasn't in a homicidal trance. Someone set him up."

"The bartender—Bo—says Troy ordered three beers but he couldn't be sure if he'd had anything prior to entering the establishment. And it wasn't the first time he'd had to call a car for Troy, or a friend. I'm sorry, Cash. I just don't see how this can—"

Glass shattered and Mae shrieked. Drywall behind Cash's head sprayed into a cloud of dusty bits. "Get down!" Cash hollered and tackled Mae to the ground, his side screeching in burning agony.

Another bullet slammed into the sofa and stuffing exploded. "Where's your radio to call in backup?" Mae asked underneath Cash's body.

"In the foyer. Stay here and I'll get it." Cash army-crawled through the living room and clenched his teeth to deal with unbearable pain. Another bullet shattered the windows in the foyer, littering the hardwood floors with glass. He'd been cut enough tonight. "Second thought. Let's get out of the house."

Mae agreed and they scurried on the floor into the kitchen, the cool tile relieving some heat from his body. "What now? We have no idea where the shooter is or if there's more than one of them."

They had to take their chances. "I'm going to swing open the door. We'll wait a beat and see if bullets fly. If not, we go straight down the deck stairs and behind the shed. We'll figure out the next steps then."

"I don't like it, but it's all we have." Mae inched backward on her hands and knees, using the kitchen counters as cover, and Cash hunched to the right of the door. He slowly reached out and touched the knob, keeping his head below the panes of the upper part of the door.

"On three," he said. "One, two, three…" He turned the knob and wrenched open the door then placed his back flush against the wall, waiting and cursing his stupid injury. After a beat of silence, he pointed to his heaving chest. "I'll go first." If someone was out there waiting to pick them off, he didn't want Mae in the line of fire. With his pulse pounding and sweat running in a steady stream down his cheeks, he pointed at the counter. "Toss me that drying towel."

Mae quickly snapped it off the counter and chucked it to him. If a shooter was lying in wait but without a scope on the gun he might shoot at any dark movement. He tossed it out the door.

No gunfire.

That only meant he might have a scope but it was now or never.

Cash inched out the back door in a crouched position, his breath ragged. Shadows hung over the backyard. A swarm of bugs hovered near the outdoor light dimly shining from the detached garage. "Come on, Mae."

Mae slipped outside with him; humidity hung like a noose around their necks. Quietly they eased from the deck. He mentally geared up for the pain that was to come and was grateful for the adrenaline pumping through his system. They darted about ten feet to the small toolshed where they took cover. Cash held his wounded area and widened his eyes as he strained to hear footsteps crunching and crackling in the pitch-black woods. As if that would help.

The hum of the air conditioning kicked on and crickets chirped alongside frogs croaking.

Maybe they were safe. Maybe the shooter had relented.

Another shot fired.

They ducked, covering their heads, and Cash felt the

pull of his stitches and sudden heat in his side. Had he popped one loose?

Nothing struck the shed. Sound came from the east side of the house. "Let's head west."

Mae nodded and they darted for the cover of the woods, Cash wincing and breathing through the pain. Though Mae was slight, her pace was fast and she didn't appear to be winded. They hustled into the trees and butted up against one of the larger ones with a massive trunk. No phones. No radio. No neighbors for eight miles.

It boiled down to a waiting game.

Mae evened out her breath to slow her heart rate, which had been pounding against her ribs. With nothing but darkness enveloping them and a thumbnail moon, shadows played tricks on her twenty-twenty vision. Cash peeked from behind the tree, calculating their next move.

The edge of his shirt was darkened, but she wasn't sure if it was from sweat or the wound. "How are you feeling?" she asked.

"I feel like a bleeding seal in the middle of an ocean with no island to take cover on."

Mae raised her eyebrows. "That's descriptive," she muttered. "I meant your stab wound."

"Oh," he said as he crouched low. "It hurts."

He could have actually used more description on that point but Mae let it go. "You know the lay of the land. What should we do?"

"I'm considering. The shooter came at us strong while we were in the house, then the shots were timed further apart outside."

Mae's heartbeat didn't slow. Whether or not some-one had returned with a vendetta or Cash was right and Lisa's real killer was after him, Mae was now heavily involved and afraid. She'd caught killers but never been on the victim's side of the road. She wouldn't let Cash know that, though. No, she'd put on her brave face and be the agent she'd trained to be. "What do you think that means?"

Cash lightly touched his wounded area. "I'm not sure but it feels strategic."

"Like he wanted to get us out of the house but if we got clipped inside—bonus points?"

Under the pale moonlight, Cash's scowl looked even more ominous. "Yeah. Like that."

"Anything in the house he might want? Guns…" She let it dangle. Cash said he'd changed and as far as petty criminal, she believed him. That was where her trust level ended, but someone from his past might not know he'd gone on the straight and narrow. They might think he would have other paraphernalia inside.

"You think someone believes I have drugs in my house." His gruff tone was all accusation and zero ques-tion. Hurt mixed with a chunk of anger in his eyes ran as transparent as spring water.

"It's not an impossible deduction," she admitted even as a tongue of heated shame licked up her cheeks. "I'm not saying *I* believe you have drugs in there. If they were pushing us out of the home on purpose then what is inside worth taking?"

Cash's jaw dropped as panic hit his eyes and he yanked her forward. "Troy's case files!"

Mae lurched into action with him, and he released her wrist as he pressed toward the house. "Think this

through, Cash! We're targets once we hit the tree line."
The killer could easily be lying in wait to pop them the
second they emerged from cover regardless of the motives behind this attack. No scenario had a safe out-
come.

"We need to make a run to the propane tank. Take
cover behind it." Cash held his side but didn't slow.

"Are you serious? Think straight, Detective!" Mae
had to work harder to keep up with Cash's long strides.
"One shot into that 250-gallon silver bullet and we're
blown to pieces. You really would be shark chum!"

Cash blinked out of his stupor and slowed then went
on high alert. "Look," he whispered.

A figure ran out the front door toward the dark country road that wound away from Cash's farmhouse.

"Let's go!" he growled and turned his direction toward the dark-clad figure. "He's got a vehicle stashed
somewhere."

Mae bit back a remark about calling in backup and
being smart and safe; it would have no effect. She tore
after him. Guess she was the backup and her imaginary
gun would be sufficient. She sneered and caught up
with him. Cash had always been impulsive and a risk
taker—behaviors that made great petty criminals and
lousy law enforcers.

Cash had reached the road, clutching his wound, by
the time Mae hit the gravel drive. *Yeah, big boy, you
were stabbed. Way to help the healing process.*

The shooter had vanished into the shadows of the
night, leaving a seething Cash. He kicked loose gravel
and growled.

"I can't believe he got away again!"

"He's smart."

"Are you saying I'm not?" His charged question fired through the glower in his eyes.

"I'm saying this was premeditated from casing your home, knowing the lay of the land and even where to park and how long it would probably take to get what he wanted—which he knew you had either by stalking or some other way—then get out and get away." Was now the time to also add that his recklessness could have gotten them killed? She'd come home to see her ailing grandmother, not to end up dead herself.

Cash wiped his brow with his corded forearm, then leaned over and took several cleansing breaths. When he stood upright, his eyes were less cloudy. "I'm sorry, Mae. I went off half-cocked. I could have gotten us both killed. Possibly tore my stiches."

"Well, at least you're aware." Her dry humor was meant to cover up the truth. She'd been, and was even now, terrified.

Cash's eyes widened and his arm shot out, then he had her wrist in his gentle hands. He ran his thumb across the tender area where he'd grabbed her. No marks. Not even sore. No need to caress it, but the apology and concern in his eyes kept her from pulling back from his touch. "I'm sorry if I hurt you."

"You didn't." Not tonight.

"I'm crazy over Troy and his situation. If he dies in prison without giving his life to Jesus… It scares me more than bullets and knives together. But putting you in the crosshairs was out of linc. I won't do it again. You have my word."

Now she more fully understood his dilemma and urgency. Mae had loved ones who hadn't given their lives to Christ either and they'd put her rusty prayer skills to use. She covered his hand with her own. "I appreciate that and I'll hold you to it." She grinned. "Now, let's see if he got those files. I saw something in his arms, I think."

The wide-open door revealed an empty coffee table. "Like I suspected. He took the paper case files."

Mae entered the house and grabbed her untouched gun on the entryway table. Cash's remained, as well. Nothing had been touched or moved out of place other than what was messed up from the gun spray.

Only the case files were missing.

"Good thing you scanned the documents onto your laptop and have them memorized. That may be the only thing saving your bacon at the SO."

He massaged the back of his neck and his jaw pulsed. "This proves it, Mae. You're right. He's been watching. Waiting. He could have stolen them before tonight, but it was when I brought you on board that he made a move."

Now there was a connection. Why steal Troy's case files unless a killer knew that she and Cash could find him? Bring real justice to Lisa and free Troy, though she didn't feel comfortable letting a wifebeater out of prison. "I need to call my unit chief and I'd like to hear Troy's story from his own lips." She didn't have to like him to do her job and bring the truth to light.

"I need to call the SO. My house is a crime scene. Unbelievable." He headed for his cell phone.

Mae called her unit chief, Colt McCoy, and he answered on the third ring. "Mae," he said through a sleep-laden voice. "Everything all right?"

He was sharper than that. "Well, how often do I call you in the middle of the night on a holiday?"

"Right. Sorry. Hold on, Georgia's asleep." Colt had

only recently married his high school sweetheart after reconnecting under murderous circumstances. She heard the quiet click of a door closing. "What's going on? Is it your grandma?"

She appreciated Colt's sensitivity.

"No, but thanks for asking. I have a dire situation here." She relayed the events that had developed hours earlier and brought him up to date on the present situation including the now possible and likely connection of the case files to Lisa Ryland's murder. "What do you think? Closed case or cold case?"

A heavy breath filtered through the line. "Email me the information when the sun comes up. There's merit to his story. Unless someone knows Cash has the files and is out to get him in trouble—though it's no reason to fire him or even suspend him, but it doesn't look good. For now, run point as if it's a reopened cold case. Hear out Troy's story and follow up with me. You know I'd bring the team out, but we've had budget cuts and can't even hire the two more necessary agents we need."

"I understand."

"Work this case with Detective Ryland as your partner. He sounds solid."

Yeah, well, she'd omitted Cash's impulsiveness and lack of judgment as well as how he'd done her dirty before. Mae was a big girl and knew how to work with men she didn't like, much less respect. "We've been spread out before." Granted they were usually in twos. "I can handle it." And she would.

"I have no doubt," Colt said, sleep now void in his tone. "If it gets hairy, call us. Stretched thin or not, we aren't going to leave you hanging."

"Thanks, Colt. I'll keep you abreast."

"Maybe just do it during business hours," he teased.

"Tell that to the bad guys."

"For real. I'll be praying for you."

"Thank you." She hung up. She forgot to ask if this still counted as vacation. A text notification beeped.

Colt.

You still have 4 days of vacation left now.

She snickered and pocketed her phone.

A rapping on the front door startled her and Cash hurried into the living room from the kitchen waving his phone. "That's what I call perfect timing." He opened the door to two sleepy-eyed detectives and two deputies—one of whom happened to be Barrett. Lovely.

He raised an eyebrow at her but said nothing.

She didn't recognize the detective wearing a wrinkly T-shirt and jeans, his CID badge loosely hung on his belt next to his SIG Sauer. But she did recognize the second detective as Shane Nicholson to whom she'd given her previous witness statement at the hospital. He was more put-together. Strawberry blonde hair combed neatly and clean-shaven. He set his dark green eyes on her.

"I don't suppose y'all need an introduction," Cash said then pointed to the rumpled-looking detective with messy blond hair, scruffy chin and cheeks, and lady-killer blue eyes.

"Mae, this is Detective Waylon Becker. We all call him 'Way' and you can too."

"Hello," Mae said quietly.

Waylon's eyes held intrigue and questions as he glanced at his watch and then at Cash. "Kinda late.

What were y'all doing when bullets fired?" The only thing his innuendo lacked was a high five with Cash.

Barrett rolled his eyes but his coming to Mae's defense was nil. He'd already assumed she wasn't returning home tonight anyway. The other deputy and detective shot Cash a knowing grin.

They knew nothing.

Humiliation raised her temperature and flushed her skin, which only aggravated her since they'd think her pink cheeks were due to embarrassment and guilt.

Cash cast a disapproving gaze among the men. "Mae is here because she's a cold case investigator with the MBI. I brought Troy's case files home—y'all know that—and she's been here going over them. Until we were used as target practice and the files were stolen. Where's the CSI?"

"On the way," Waylon said as he surveyed the damage. "We'll secure the scene, though."

"What's your take?" The deputy standing next to Barrett pointed to Mae. His badge told her his name was Anderson. "Billy," he introduced himself.

"I'll know more once I talk to Cash's brother tomorrow, but as of right now it's an open, unsolved homicide."

No one disagreed out of clear respect for Cash, but Mae studied their faces—including Barrett's. They didn't believe Troy was innocent. Waylon Becker might. But she wasn't sure.

"Let's get to work," Barrett said. "I'll take east-to-west perimeter. Billy, you take north-to-south. If he left something, we'll find it." He paused at the door and caught Mae's eye, mouthing, "Are you good?"

She nodded. He gave her a once-over to be sure she

wasn't physically hurt then left. CSI showed up and the house filled with further levels of testosterone. Oh joy.

Cash ushered Mae into a private corner in the kitchen. "Sorry about where their minds went, Mae. Men can be real jerks."

"Say it isn't so," Mae remarked with more force than intended. "I'm well aware of how men think and behave. I can take care of myself."

He nodded.

"But…I appreciate you setting them straight on my purpose for being here. That was…stand-up of ya." Most men would have let it go and enjoyed the innuendo, and Cash had nothing to gain by setting the record straight. She'd already agreed to work the case.

Surprise lit in his eyes. "No problem. I'm well aware of why you're here. And it ain't me. It's justice. So… what did your unit chief say?"

She gave him the rundown and he seemed pleased.

"I'll make sure we see Troy tomorrow. If anyone can ferret out what truly went down, it's you. I've never met anyone smarter. And that's not flattery. That's truth."

His touching words landed on the soft part of her heart, but she fought them from settling there and knocking her sideways. Mae had checks and balances. Cash was a heartbreaker—no, heart-ripper. Check. She had to keep that at the forefront of everything said and done. Balanced.

"Justice will be served." And that's all she would be offering up on Cash's plate.

THREE

Mae yawned as they finished passing through security and signed logbooks. The smell of the Mississippi State Penitentiary was stale and sterile. Drab grays, tans and creams. The correctional officer led them to a closet-sized room to wait for Troy. The room was warm and dimly lit. If they waited too long, she'd doze off. Three hours of sleep last night wasn't nearly enough.

She'd met Cash at his house, driven him to the shop where he'd picked up his unmarked unit with fresh tires and hit the road, passing through for a biscuit and coffee at a nearby Hardee's. The smell of butter and yeast had filled her senses and her empty stomach.

She peeked at Cash. His minimal sleep hadn't affected his looks. Shame. Skipping a shave and throwing on a pair of black dress pants, fitted white dress shirt with his sleeves rolled up to the elbows in this wilting heat did nothing to sour his physique.

"Did you pop a stitch last night?" she asked.

"No. Thankfully. I rebandaged it and so far, I haven't had any bleeding." He raised his arm to glance down at his wound.

Mae tried to ignore the way his biceps stretched his soft shirt. There was a faint scar near his elbow.

Mae dusted invisible crumbs off her high-waisted khaki pants and opened the scanned digital file Cash had emailed her. "Did you like Lisa?" She needed insight and talking about the case was smarter than gawking at Cash's sinewy physique.

"Lisa was great and I wish she wouldn't have gotten involved with Troy the way he was, but he had good moments. She was smart and ambitious. She went to school to be a court reporter and made a nice living."

"Let's say Troy didn't kill her—"

"He didn't," Cash insisted.

"Okay. Could her job have connected her to someone who would want to hurt her?" She flipped to the photos of Lisa Ryland's body postmortem. "It was a personal attack." She'd been beaten especially in the face as if the killer didn't want to see it or have her see him. "And also rage." The amount of brutal damage was overwhelming. Multiple breaks. Fractures. Lacerations. "The front door had been unlocked when first responders arrived on that following Monday when she missed work. The DA argued that Troy used his spare key to let himself in—which he still possessed. But it's possible that Lisa knew her killer and allowed him access into her home. Or someone else had a key." The evidence against Troy was severely damaging. Mae would have found him guilty if she'd been on the jury.

Mae checked her watch. "What's taking so long?"

"I don't know. Usually I sit on the other side of the glass and he comes right in. Never had to question him as a detective."

"I've been here but I don't remember waiting this

long. Most often, when new evidence comes to light in a cold case, our suspect is already doing time for another similar crime." She squirmed and the walls felt like they were closing in on her. "I hate tight spaces. Have since I was a kid."

Cash studied her and cocked his head. "Close your eyes and breathe deeply."

She followed his instructions and thought of wide-open spaces.

"I remember when you told me about that time you were shoved into your locker junior year. I don't mind enclosed areas but don't put me near a wasps' nest. I'm done for. Got into a nest when I was a kid and nearly died. I'm not allergic but the number of stings was enough to cause damage and serious pain."

"I hate those too. Anything that inflicts pain, I'm not for." She grinned, opened her eyes and frowned. "Could he be in solitary?"

"He doesn't cause trouble. He dried out in prison and has been to a few church services officiated by a local church. Wish he'd make the decision to trust Jesus, but he's been holding back. Not sure why." He rubbed his palms on his thighs. "I'm getting a little worried."

Mae huffed. Concern was beginning to eat at her too. "I'll check. It's like an oven in this room and I'm getting cranky anyway." She reached for the door as a correctional officer opened it, startling her. "Oh, I was just coming to see if there was a problem." She peered behind the barrel-chested officer with a slick head, and guns blazing on both upper arms. No Troy. "Is there a problem?"

"I'm afraid there's been an incident."

Cash was on his feet and to the door in a flash. "What

kind of incident? Where's my brother?" His voice was low and confrontational as if he were ready to rumble.

"Your brother was involved in an altercation about fifteen minutes ago. He was stabbed by another inmate while working in the laundry room. It was severe—"

"Is he alive?" Cash's tone was eerily quiet and frightening. His knuckles whitened as his fists remained clenched.

"He's being rushed into surgery. That's all I know about his condition," the officer said with diplomacy.

Mae stepped up. One of them had to be levelheaded but this was unsettling and likely not a coincidence. "Do they have the offending inmate in custody?"

His tough face softened and apology bloomed in his dark gray eyes. "It happened in a camera's blind spot but it's being investigated. We have a log of inmates in the laundry area, but it's possible someone slipped inside unnoticed."

"Unbelievable!" Cash bellowed. "Which hospital?"

Cash wasn't thinking straight or didn't care. Prisons weren't allowed to inform anyone of the inmate's location when treatment had to be done off-site. "Will he be transported back here for recovery?" Mae asked.

"I want to see the warden," Cash said. "Now."

Mae sighed and the officer nodded then closed the door behind them.

"What happened to not going off half-cocked? You'll get us nowhere by brutish demands and rearing up like a bull ready to buck from the gate." She paused and laid a hand on his arm. "You have every reason to be concerned and even afraid. But try to shake the big brother and be the detective. Cool. Calm. Steady." Getting in a state of panic wasn't going to help anyone.

Cash relaxed, leaned over his knees, inhaled a few cleansing breaths then peered up at her with a smirk that bordered on toe curling. "I feel like I keep saying sorry."

She gave him a stern expression like a teacher to a student who'd launched a spit wad. "Well, that's because you keep doing things that require apologies."

"I probably ought to stop that."

Did he know how cute he was? And should she be thinking about that at a time like this? No. "That's the best idea you've had since we walked through the prison doors. Keep those coming." She had him disarmed and calm. She was anything but.

Mae coaxed Cash into the plastic chair and stood between him and the door in case he decided to buck out of the stall after all. "We're the law. We have access that average family members don't. But we have to play nice. Can you do that, Cash? For Troy's sake? He needs you."

Cash hung his head and pawed his face. "I can do it. For Troy."

"Yes," she said soothingly. "For Troy." His muscles relaxed and his neck lost its bloodred hue. "Nice and calm. Cool and collected. Cash is in control," she reminded him.

"Mae, you have a knack for this. Anybody ever tell you that?" His gaze met hers, and he appeared so boyish and lost she wanted to stroke his hair. Like the little boy who'd gotten lost on Fourth of July. Cash looked exactly like that.

"Oh, I've been told a time or two I'm good at calming a tense situation or person." Which was great except that no one was calming her. This was bad. Really bad, and she couldn't say it or even let on that she was borderline freaking out. Cash would go off the rails.

"What if the killer got to the inmate who tried to kill Troy?" Cash asked. Now he was thinking like a detective.

"The thought did cross my mind—"

The door gently opened and the same correctional officer stood at the threshold. "Warden Royce will see you. Follow me." They followed him to Warden Royce's office, which was quite spacious, and Mae could breathe again.

A tall slender man with a shock of white hair and wiry eyebrows to match welcomed them inside and to take seats across from his desk.

"I'm sorry, Detective Ryland. My team is surveying tapes now to find who might have done this. Due to the blind spot, I'm not sure what we'll be able to discover. Once Troy makes it through surgery and recovery, he'll be transported back here and kept in our infirmary to fully recuperate."

Cash's jaw ticked. "Thank you. Can you tell me if Troy has had any prior run-ins with anyone or what might have caused this one?"

Warden Royce rubbed his stubbly chin. "Troy is a model inmate. He keeps his head down—which is wise—and does what he's told. He seems to be well-liked. Sometimes these things, unfortunately, happen."

"But you don't think so, do you?" Mae asked. It was in Warden Royce's eyes. Puzzlement. Irritation.

"No. I think Troy might have been targeted but I don't know why."

Mae had a couple of guesses. They were onto something big. Someone.

"Y'all are welcome to wait in the lounge until you hear any news. I'll have an officer near to keep you updated."

"Can we help with looking at those security tapes? It'll keep us from going stir-crazy." Cash waited, his foot tapping on the floor.

"Of course. I'm happy to extend you the courtesy. Officer Jones will escort you to the security office." With that they were dismissed and followed the giant officer to the security level and offices where four guards were viewing tapes.

Hopefully, they'd find Troy's attacker and get some answers before it was too late. If a hit had been put out on Troy, the killer wasn't going to let him recover. And he wasn't going to stop with Cash's brother. He'd targeted Cash and Mae too.

An hour had ticked by like almost-crystallized honey eking out of a plastic bear. The helplessness clawed Cash's bones and vibrated against his skin. He had no way of being near Troy or even knowing what hospital he was in for surgery. He'd called Mom and broken the news, which sent her into tears. She wasn't a bad mother. She loved Cash and Troy as much as a mother working to the bone and carrying a huge weight in the form of an alcoholic husband could love a couple of rowdy boys. He'd promised to keep her posted and instructed her not to worry—he'd worry for them both. And pray. But even through his silent prayers that begged God to spare his brother's life and use it for Troy's ears to hear saving grace knocking on the door to his crusty, angry heart, Cash couldn't deny the heavy anchor of guilt that dropped around his own heart for his part in Troy's downward trajectory.

It's a beer, Troy. Don't be such a baby.

That had been Troy's first taste at twelve and Cash had goaded him into it.

We're not gonna get caught, Troy. Stop being a little girl.

That had been the first time Cash had shown a thirteen-year-old Troy how to lift a candy bar from a convenience store without getting caught dead to rights. Candy bars had escalated to smokes, booze and anything else they'd felt entitled to snatch.

But he'd never taught Troy how to hit a girl. That was where the line was drawn. Cash had been a big drinker but never had it leeched to his soul like Troy or Dad. He'd never understood the kind of tug it had and how it affected their moods, allowing them to strike a loved one—a woman. Cash regretted never intervening between Dad and Mom when his father had gone on a bender and shoved her around. He'd been afraid.

Mae broke him from the agonizing memories. "Back it up," she quipped and pointed at the monitor. She was incredible. Always in control and fluid. She was everything he wished he could be. Smart. Insightful. Steady.

Did the woman ever break a sweat? Tiny but a powerhouse.

Cash zeroed in and focused on the black-and-white feed.

"That guy," she stated. "He wasn't in the employees' line but he breezes by and then out after Troy's stabbing when the frenzy broke out. I want to talk to him," she said with a glint in her eye. Cash tried to tear his eyes away from her, but it wasn't easy.

"Nice catch, Agent," one of the officers said and left the security station.

"Yeah," Cash said with proud grin. "Nice catch."

"Just doing my job." She sat back and stared at the screen. She'd never been comfortable receiving compliments. Even now, she seemed irritated by it. Well, too bad. When warranted, Cash was all about dishing them out. He'd gone most of his life starved for a pat on the back or an atta-boy. Encouragement and appreciation were valuable and went a long way.

In ten minutes, they were led to a private questioning room with inmate and possible perpetrator Tommy Leonard, a scroungy, long-haired slug with malice in his eyes and a hardened jaw. Cash had seen this look before. Tommy had nothing to lose or gain by giving up any information. They'd get squat from him.

Twenty minutes of interrogation proved Cash right. Tommy Leonard was doing fifty-four years for capital murder. No finagling or deals would offer him incentive to admit to the crime or share useful information. Either he was there to help whoever did it or he committed the crime, but he had no blood on his clothes.

"We don't need you to admit anything, Tommy," Mae said. "All we need is to connect you to Troy. And I've always been good at the connecting-dots game."

Tommy's pug face scrunched as he hurled an insult at Mae. She didn't flinch and waved as the guard led him back to solitary confinement.

Another guard opened the door. "Troy's out of surgery and stable. He'll be transported back in an hour."

Cash released a pent-up breath he wasn't even aware he'd been holding and his knees nearly buckled. *Thank You, God.*

"See," Mae said. "Everything's gonna be okay."

Cash wasn't quite as optimistic. "Yeah," he said anyway. "When we get back in town we need to look into Tommy Leonard and see if we can connect him to Troy or to Lisa."

She gave him a friendly smack on the back. "Now you're talking."

After three cups of coffee and endless pacing, they were allowed to see Troy. The doctor noted he was groggy but coherent.

Troy was frail and drained of color as he lay on the hospital bed draped in white. His eyes fluttered and then his sight landed on Mae and his brow creased.

"Hey, bro, looks like stabbing is running in the family." Cash chuckled and Troy smiled but clearly didn't get the joke. "Can you talk?"

"Water?" he rasped and Mae poured a small foam cup full for him and helped him sip. For detesting a man who she deep-down believed killed his ex-wife, she extended that straw like an olive branch.

"Did you see your attacker, Troy?" Mae asked.

He removed the straw from his lips. "Thank you," he said. "Who are you?"

"This is Mae Vogel. She's an agent with the MBI cold case homicide unit. She's reopened your case, bro. We're gonna get the real killer." His voice had clogged with emotion but he didn't mind. This was emotional.

"Thank you," he whispered and sipped again. "I didn't see him." He gained more power in his voice, but it still sounded muffled and raspy.

"Does the name Tommy Leonard ring a bell?"

Troy shook his head.

Cash explained what had happened and that his attacker might have been Tommy. "We'll make sure you have protective custody. Mae is here to listen to your side of the story—the truth."

Slowly, through many pauses, Troy shared about that night and about his marriage to Lisa.

"I know I was a bad husband and I hated myself. I wanted to change. I still do."

"I'm glad you know you should," Mae said. She'd listened stoically. Cash couldn't read her at all.

"I didn't kill her, Miss Vogel. I just want out of here."

Mae flipped the page on her yellow legal pad. She'd scribbled dozens of notes during Troy's statement. "Can you tell me if Lisa was seeing someone else while you were separated or after the divorce? Could she have had an affair?"

Troy closed his eyes. He was tired and needed rest. "If she was seeing anyone, she was keeping it a secret from me, including an affair. And you know small towns—not much gets by unnoticed." His breathing deepened.

"Let him sleep," Mae said. "I've heard enough. With everything that has ensued since last night, I tend to believe Troy has been framed. Someone wanted to kill Lisa and Troy was an easy fall guy. The question is why did someone want Lisa Ryland dead? I'm going to need to do the victimology. If I can answer the why then that will most likely lead us to the who."

Cash didn't want to leave Troy.

Mae gripped his biceps. "The best thing we can do is let him recover and work the case."

She must have read his mind, known his thoughts.

"I know. It's just hard."

Mae looked at a sleeping Troy. "It is. But they'll monitor him. We have a job to do and the sooner we do it, the sooner he comes home and the real killer reaps justice."

Cash patted Troy's leg and caught Mae's eye. There was so much he wanted to say but couldn't. Words had never been his thing.

Her sticking around meant a lot. "You're right."

After talking with the warden one last time, they hit the road headed toward Willow Banks. They passed through a drive-through and ate greasy burgers and fries, which hit the spot. About ten miles from Willow Banks, his cell phone rang.

The district attorney's office. Wayne Furlow. He answered. "Detective Ryland."

"Hi, Detective. It's Janine at District Attorney Furlow's office. Can you come by around three and talk to him about a case you're currently working?"

Probably the Rankin case Wayne was prosecuting. Ought to be a slam dunk. Everyone in the bar saw Rankin bash the victim's head with a broken beer bottle. He checked the time. "I should be able to make that, Janine. Thanks for calling." He hung up and relayed the message to Mae. "I'll take you to your car so you can get home. It's been an exhausting day."

Her face said she didn't want to go home. Odd. She'd always lived in a nice upper-class home with a basketball goal out front and big flower beds. Cash had been envious of her upbringing. But maybe he didn't know everything. One thing he'd learned from working at the SO was that nothing was as it appeared to be. Not crime scenes, homes or even people. There was the part they wanted a person to see, the part they lived in front of their family and the secret places. Wonder what secrets the Vogel house kept?

"I'll go with you actually. Before Lisa transferred to chancery court, she worked circuit court. Wayne Furlow is the DA so he might have personal knowledge."

"He's going to be miffed that the case is reopened. He prosecuted Troy." That hadn't been easy. Cash typically worked with Wayne to see a criminal take their consequences. But he hadn't been on Wayne's side in Troy's case and had been vocal about it. Since then, they'd patched up things by agreeing to disagree on Troy's innocence. "I'd have thought if he had pertinent information about Lisa he'd have already factored that into the case."

"The case was winnable without personal details and it's possible he knows something he doesn't realize he knows because he hasn't been asked."

True.

"Would he be the type to withhold pertinent information to win a case?" Mae asked.

Cash pulled off the ramp that led into Willow Banks. "I don't think so. I mean there've been some rumors about his relationships. Whirlwind Wayne. He doesn't stick with a woman for long. But, when it comes to his profession, he's been stellar. Word is he's going to run for attorney general in two years. I think he could win. Not saying he has my vote, after Troy, though." He chuckled. "I know he was doing his job, which is to present the evidence. It wrinkled, though."

Mae cut him a side eye. He must have missed a word. He pulled from his memory box but couldn't make it work. Nothing to do but let it go and feel the fiery flames of humiliation creep up his neck.

"Understandable. I imagine it did *rankle*." She peered out the window. "Construction going on at the office?"

Wayne's office was directly across the street from the courthouse in the county administration building. Built about ten years ago, it was tall with round windows lining the rotund front of the building. The American flag, Mississippi State flag and a green flag—letting residents know the air quality was good today—hung on gleaming silver poles front and center.

"They're doing some expansions." He parked in the back lot and they strode into the work zone, dodging orange cones and ducking yellow tape. Construction crew must be on a break. No signs of people and no racket going on. They entered the side door, the smell of fresh drywall and paint nailing his senses.

The gaps in the ceiling revealed wiring, insulation and metal rafters. Scaffolding had been butted up against the wall and plastic draped the tile flooring. Scuffles sounded above. Maybe someone was working after all.

"What are they adding?" Mae asked.

"Planning-commission offices and a new conference center. Tax dollars hard at work," he quipped and moved down the hallway. Scraping and dragging thundered above and the hairs on his neck stood at attention. He paused and surveyed overhead. Surely, they wouldn't allow traffic in these hallways if it was unsafe. But it didn't sound secure.

Mae frowned. "I heard that. Like furniture being moved. The ceiling is stable, right?"

Furlow's office was in the hall on the left. "As far as—"

A crack ripped through the hallway and Mae gasped.

Cash shoved Mae out of the way as heavy scaffolding collapsed. He dived, but the metal clipped his back leg and an excruciating pain tore through his right side clear to his brain. Drywall, ceiling tiles and debris rained down in a foggy cloud.

Mae shrieked and ran into the swirl of drywall dust. "Cash!"

Rumbling overhead drew her attention and she shielded her eyes and squinted.

"I'm pinned," he said through gritted teeth.

Hurdling chunks of scaffolding and junk that had fallen from the ceiling, she reached him and knelt. "I'm going to lift this off you then you need to drag yourself out." She grabbed the edge of the metal equipment, ground her teeth and pushed upward, straining. It didn't budge.

"Go get help," Cash said through the throbbing and stabs of pain in his leg and the wound he'd already incurred.

Mae looked overhead. "I don't believe that was an accident. If I leave something worse may happen." She gripped the edge of the scaffolding again and dug in her heels. "On three," she bellowed. "One…two…" She put her legs into it and the scaffolding budged. "Three," she said through a strenuous groan as she raised the heavy equipment enough for him to slide out his leg before it toppled back to the floor. He scooted to the wall, rested his head against it. His leg was bleeding and already darkened by the bruising but he didn't think it was broken and he wouldn't need stitches—again.

She jumped the scaffolding and slid beside him, observing the damage. "Can you stand?"

Cash gritted his teeth at the intense throb and ache, but managed to stand on his good leg and slowly apply weight to the injured one. He could put pressure on it. Mild relief.

Mae clutched her chest and said a thankful prayer. "Come on. Let's get to Furlow's office. Stick to the walls this time." She grabbed his arm and draped it around her as they cautiously inched along toward the DA's office.

"I can walk by myself, Mae."

"Well, let's not take any more chances. That was a close one. Shouldn't we call in backup? Have the ceiling checked out?" Her bravado faltered and her voice cracked. She'd been rattled, scared. So had he.

He should have gone with his instincts when he first heard the racket overhead. Now the question was who would know they were coming to see Furlow at three o'clock and how long had they been hiding? "I'd say whoever it was tore out pretty quick, but we can get forensics up there for evidence." He made the call as they hobbled into Wayne Furlow's office and were met with Janine's wide eyes. "What on earth?" she asked.

"Hey, Janine, could you—" Wayne stepped into the reception area in his expensive navy suit, with tidy hair and a fresh-shaven face. "Detective Ryland? What happened to you?" He glanced at Mae, who was covered with white drywall dust from head to toe. He switched his gaze back to Cash. "And what are you doing here this time of day?"

"You wanted to see me," Cash said.

Wayne's brow furrowed. "No, I didn't."

FOUR

Cash passed Mae the sticky note Janine assumed was from Wayne. To him, it was all chicken scratch. Mae frowned. "Does this look like your handwriting?"

"Who are you again?" Wayne asked and eyed the note.

Mae introduced herself with clipped professionalism. "We're reopening Lisa Ryland's case."

"Cash, please expound." Wayne's neck flushed red and he loosened his flashy silver tie.

"Troy didn't kill Lisa. We think the real killer may have left that note to set a trap and lure us here." He pointed to the sticky note for emphasis.

Wayne's cheeks flinched and he licked his lips. "Janine, did you see anyone enter the office? Wander down the halls?"

Janine shook her head and a mass of red curls bounced around her face. Her wide brown eyes held a measure of panic. "I didn't see anyone. But the note wasn't here before I left for lunch." Her bottom lip quivered. "The writing is close enough I just assumed you'd written it."

Wayne frowned, then softened and rubbed her shoulders. Cash found that a tad unprofessional, but Janine didn't seem uncomfortable. "Janine, none of this is your fault. Or mine."

Mae studied the two with an eyebrow raised, then focused on Wayne. "Can I see something you did actually write, Mr. Furlow?"

Wayne released Janine's shoulders and flashed Mae one of those grins with creased dimples that earned him jury votes. Mae didn't respond with a verdict Wayne had intended and he frowned as he handed her a document he'd signed.

She compared the writing, then showed it to Cash. At first glance it appeared the same, but upon closer examination, Cash saw a few differences. "It's close enough that whoever wrote it is a pro or familiar with your handwriting. Either way, they knew it needed to resemble yours or it would be questioned."

"And they either watched and waited for you to leave, Janine," Mae said, "or they knew your lunchtime break. Do you leave the same time each day?"

Janine shook her head again. "No. I mean I try to go between twelve and two when court typically breaks but some days are hectic. You think it's someone we know? I can't believe someone I'm friendly with could do this." She looked to Wayne as if he had answers or possibly comfort.

He patted her shoulder but his jaw worked overtime. Had he realized his mistake by putting the wrong man in prison? "We don't know who it was. It doesn't take a rocket scientist to observe when court is in session and out and when we take lunches. Anyone could have dressed like a construction worker or even simply ducked in and out. We don't have cameras. But one thing we do know is there's no concrete evidence that connects to Troy or warrants reopening this case. On what basis did you reopen it?" he asked Mae, all flirtation gone.

Mae explained the details from Cash's stabbing to the attempted murder of Troy. "The case files being stolen piqued our interest most. I'm pursuing it—to wherever or whomever it leads."

"It'll circle back to Troy, Agent Vogel." Smugness had replaced friendliness. Wayne returned his attention to Cash. "The evidence against Troy was airtight, Cash. The detectives—your colleagues and friends—did a thorough job."

"Let's say Troy did kill Lisa," Mae said. "The fact that we're poking around in the case has someone's dander up. Maybe it's not her killer—Troy allegedly did that—but it's someone who has secrets to protect, and they're dark enough to motivate them to stop us before we begin."

Wayne pinched the bridge of his nose. "What do you need me to do?"

"Do you have any personal knowledge that might offer us additional insight into Lisa? She worked circuit court for a few years. How close were the two of you?" Cash asked.

Wayne frowned. "Lisa was married during her time here."

"Right. But the question still stands, Wayne."

"No, we weren't intimate. We had a professional relationship—though I was aware of the domestic issues. So, did it hurt my feelings to try the case against Troy? No, Cash. It didn't. However, it should hurt your feelings in attempting to overturn the conviction. He's in prison because the abuse escalated. He was angry she'd left him, divorced him and was moving forward with a life that excluded him. If he couldn't have her then no one could. End of story."

Wayne might as well have kicked him in the gut. Cash wasn't negating Lisa's death or ignoring the abuse she'd endured at the hands of his brother. He wanted justice for Lisa as much as anyone. He'd loved her like a sister. "I tried to help her."

"Well, you're not helping her now. I'm sorry for the near tragedy you experienced today, and if I can help find who perpetrated this new crime—you have my full backing. But as far as Lisa is concerned, I did my job and I sleep well at night."

Mae thanked him and followed Cash into the hall.

Mae fanned her face as they exited the building into the blazing heat. "I don't like him and I certainly don't trust him. But I doubt he climbed into the ceiling to drop scaffolding on us. He doesn't seem the type to get his hands dirty. However, he could have skewed his handwriting, left us the note and hired someone to take us out. Your DA has everything to lose if this case gets overturned. He put away an innocent man. That could be the kiss of death in his run for attorney general."

Cash opened the car door for Mae and she slid into the passenger seat. He hobbled inside and started the engine and the air conditioning. "Wayne isn't on my favorites list either, but I'm having a hard time believing he'd go to those lengths."

"I need to know more about Lisa, and Tommy Leonard. If we can connect him to Troy or her, we may be closer to finding a common link. Whoever stabbed Troy had to have received an order from someone who knew we were investigating—or that you were. If Tommy was given incentive to murder Troy then there has to be a paper trail. Someone visited or called him."

"Or went through another inmate to relay the message. Someone smart wouldn't want to be on the call or visitor logs. We need to see who Tommy hung out with in prison—including his cell mate—and look at the visitor and call logs, but first we need to see if there's a direct link to Tommy and Troy."

"Smart thinking, Cash."

Cash's chest swelled. That was twice she'd called him smart. But she didn't know the truth.

Mae tapped her fingernail on the side of the car door as he drove them across town to the SO. Mae's phone rang and she dug through her purse and answered, "Hey, Mom…I'm fine…Yes. What time?…I'll be home…Love you too." She ended the call. "Moms never stop checking in on their kids, do they?"

Cash grinned. "My mom calls almost every night and since she's gotten better at texting, I might get a heart or happy face emoji. She's a good woman."

Mae sighed. "My mom is too. She tries."

"What do you mean?" Cash asked. From all appearances, Mae had the perfect childhood, family and home.

She waved him off. "Nothing."

It was something. And it seemed like she wanted to talk about it or she wouldn't have brought it up. "My mom wasn't much involved with us growing up. Not because she didn't care but because she had to work more than one job to keep us clothed and fed. My dad drank. He could get mean sometimes. I'd hear Mom crying late at night, but if I ever asked her what was wrong she simply dried it up and told me, *Sometimes girls cry, Cash.* I hated that. I felt like guys shouldn't make girls cry to begin with."

Cash glanced her way at the stoplight. Looked like she might tear up right now. Had he made her cry? He surely had when he'd robbed her of the coveted spot of valedictorian.

"I'm sorry, Mae," he said. "I'm sorry if I made you cry. I told myself I'd never do that—like my dad did. Guess I was more like him than I wanted to be. We don't always learn by what we're taught but what we caught in their behavior then imitated. I've been working for a while to unlearn some of those things. I'm praying Troy will wake up and realize he has a lot of unlearning too."

Mae blinked and swallowed hard. "Thank you." This time it felt like a genuine sentiment. "I saw my mom cry once. And my dad told her crying wasn't going to solve it. I don't know what the 'it' was but I learned that crying—at least in front of my dad—was weakness. So I get that whole learning what's caught over taught."

He pulled into the SO. "Grace goes a long way. I could have been mad at my mom for the lack of nurturing we received. But she was doing the best she could with what she had at the moment. Some days, I think she was just trying to survive."

Mae unbuckled her seat belt, but stared into her lap, lost in thought. "I think most women are just trying to survive, Cash. Living in a man's world isn't easy."

Cash wasn't naive. This line of work often was a man's world. It wasn't right. He had many female colleagues he'd rather put his trust in. Teri for one. But Mae's hard line of thinking went back further than her occupation. He'd heard about what happened to her in high school her junior year. Landon Murry had stolen a pair of her underwear from the girls' locker room and spread rumors about how he retrieved it. Cash never believed it. Mae had been a sweet girl and wouldn't have given Landon the time of day.

Cash had related to humiliation and bullying. It was one of the reasons he'd chosen Mae to tutor him. Even if he'd messed up, she wouldn't have made fun of him.

"Guys can be real jerks, Mae. But not every man will be." He removed the keys from the ignition. "Not that we aren't prone to disappointing people. We're human." He shrugged. "Grace goes a long way," he repeated.

She grunted as if she didn't believe him. "I'll let you know when that becomes truth in my personal experience."

With her bias—including him—she wouldn't see the truth about some men being honorable because she didn't want to and there was no point in trying to convince her, but it struck a nerve. He'd done a jerky thing but he wasn't a jerk—not anymore. "Let's go look at Tommy Leonard's rap sheet." He hoped they'd find some connection or they were at a dead end. They had no real proof Tommy had attempted to murder Troy.

She grabbed her purse and closed the car door, followed him through the back entrance.

All he needed was Mae's help to free his brother. Then she could go on believing he was the bad guy. So be it. What did he care?

Except there was a scraping against his bones that wouldn't go away.

Mae held up Tommy Leonard's file. The guy was complete slime and had revolved in and out of prison for years until this last stint that kept him there. "Look at the name listed as his defense attorney."

Cash glanced at the paper and for a second looked like he might throw up. Was he sick? He'd been quiet since they came inside. Likely due to her statement about men being jerks. She hadn't excluded him.

She felt the twinge of guilt from being harsh. Presently, Cash had proved himself to be kind, respectful and protective. If he hadn't pushed her out of harm's way first, it would have been Mae pinned by the scaffolding and with her small frame the injuries could have been severe or even fatal. A chill rippled down her spine at that thought.

Her earlier behavior was shameful. His heartfelt and passionate words coupled with the pain in his eyes couldn't be dismissed as great acting or a prelude to underlying motives.

It had moved her more than she wanted to be moved. So much she'd almost cried. She couldn't remember a single time a man had been that genuine toward her concerning a fault he'd committed, a hurt he'd inflicted or the pure honesty in revealing something as personal as his growing-up years. His mom told him girls sometimes cried. Her father told her crying would get her nowhere and to suck it up.

Cash didn't mind a woman crying but he didn't want to be the reason for it. If that wasn't unadulterated honesty, she didn't know what was. She wasn't sure what to do with that other than tuck it away and focus on the case.

"Cash, look at the name."

His neck flushed and he slowly retrieved the file and perused it. "Huh."

"Just huh?" She took the file back. "He has the same defense attorney as your brother. I'd think that warrants more than a *huh*. Try *oh uh-uh*. Harrison Trout defended both of these men. If he's on either of their visitor or call logs it would make sense. We have connected dots."

"Why would Harrison Trout want Troy dead—if the hit came from him? What's his motive?"

That was the big question. "Would Harrison know you were trying to get Troy freed?"

"Troy has maintained his innocence this entire time and I've talked to Harrison about trying to appeal, but he said they didn't have anything to take to a judge. I told him I'd find something. So yeah, he knows."

Mae rubbed her chin as possibilities rattled around. "Would he have any reason to want Troy in prison?"

Cash shook his head. "He didn't even know Troy until we hired him. He was better than a public defender—in our opinion—and less than some Memphis attorneys. I never felt he tried too hard. But I'm biased."

"I want to read through the transcripts before we talk to him. I'll be more prepared. Guess that will be my bedtime reading. Do we have time to visit chancery court and talk to coworkers and anyone who knew Lisa well?"

Cash checked the time. "It's pushing four. If we move quickly we might be able to reach a few. But everything shuts down at five and sometimes before four if a judge is done."

Mae grabbed her purse. "Let's go. What we can't cover today, we'll hit tomorrow along with Harrison Trout. I'll be up-to-date on the transcripts by morning."

"You gonna sleep at all?"

"As my grandma Rose says, *I'll sleep when I'm dead*," she said as they blew through the SO hall toward the back of the building. As they rounded the corner, they smacked into Cash's CID colleague, Waylon Becker.

"Whoa now," he said with a grin. "Is that any way to be moving after a stabbing and scaffolding injury?"

Cash chuckled. "We're on our way to chancery court. Talk to Lisa's friends and colleagues."

Waylon glanced at Mae. "Rumor has it you saved his bacon today. You don't look big enough to lift a loaf of bread let alone heavy equipment. Nicely done, Agent."

Mae was prepared to stand her ground, but Waylon appeared to be giving a legit compliment. "Thank you."

"Maybe to celebrate, I could buy you coffee sometime."

And there was the underlying motive. "I'm here to work, but thanks."

Waylon cocked his head. "Well, if you get thirsty and need some caffeine, offer stands."

Cash bristled and clenched his jaw but said nothing.

"We have to go," Mae said, dismissing Waylon. The man wasn't leering and didn't give her a creepy vibe but she was here professionally. They strode toward Cash's unmarked vehicle.

"If you were interested in having coffee with Way—he's a decent guy." His words were encouraging; his tone was anything but. Why had Cash bristled?

"I'm not interested. I meant it when I said I was here on a case." She yanked open the passenger door and plopped onto the hot leather seat.

"Noted." He backed out and drove across town to

chancery court. Inside, they met a clerk who informed them that most of the chancellors were gone for the day.

It was getting close to five anyway and Mae had promised Mom she'd be home in time for dinner. She was cooking her favorite—roast, baby carrots and new potatoes with fresh yeast rolls.

"I guess we can come back tomorrow." Cash frowned. "I'd hoped we could make some headway."

"Me too."

"Mae? Mae Vogel?"

Mae turned and beamed. "Lilith Freedman!" She rushed forward to the deputy and hugged her. "How long has it been?"

"Let's not talk about how many years have passed. It makes me feel old." Lilith laughed and her deep-set blue eyes sparkled. She looked great. She'd always been tall, and she was fit. Mae worked out daily to keep strong but Lilith took it to a new level.

"You look amazing and you're a deputy!" She wasn't surprised Lilith had gone into law enforcement. It had been Lilith who'd rescued her from the locker one of the football players had shoved her into after she'd decked Landon Murry for stealing her underwear and touting lewd, nasty rumors about her and how he'd acquired them.

"Yeah. Went into the navy after high school and here I am. I'm Chancellor Pendergrass's bailiff. What about you? You here for divorce court? Only Chancellor Sharp is still in session."

"Oh. No. I'm not married. I'm a cold case agent with the MBI."

Lilith nodded. "That makes sense with you being here with Cash. How are you doing, Detective?"

Cash dipped his chin in a greeting. "Good. We were actually here to talk with Judge Vickie Pendergrass."

"We're reopening Lisa Ryland's case," Mae offered.

"Oh okay. I knew Lisa pretty well. She was professional and kind to everyone." Lilith glanced at Cash.

"I'm going to go see if I can talk with Judge Sharp if there's time."

"He prefers the title *chancellor*," Lilith said. "Even if they are synonymous. *Chancellor* sounds more prestigious."

"Noted. Excuse me," he said and disappeared down the hall.

"We should catch up," Lilith said, "grab coffee or lunch. How long will you be in town?"

"Well, it was supposed to be a week of vacation then back to Batesville. But now that the case is reopened, I'm not sure how long I'll be here. Let's definitely get lunch, though." She peered down the empty hall. "Now that Cash is gone, be real with me. What do you know and what do you think?"

Lilith frowned. "I know it was an ugly divorce. Chancellor Sharp presided over it. Troy blew a gasket and Billy—Anderson—he's a deputy who also fills in as a bailiff when necessary—had to subdue him. Chancellor Sharp pronounced him in contempt and he spent a night in jail. I don't know why it went south."

Interesting. They didn't have kids to fight over in a custody battle, but a lot of divorces ended in sour grapes.

"Lisa worked in Chancellor Pendergrass's courtroom where I work as bailiff. She had sad eyes. We all knew Troy had been in trouble with the law. Vickie talked to her once about Troy. I'm not sure how it went, but a few months later Lisa filed for divorce so maybe whatever she said stuck. And to be honest, I'm pretty sure I talked to her anonymously about the abuse."

Mae cocked her head. "How so?"

"Vickie opened a domestic violence safe house about ten years ago and a crisis hotline, which is all run by volunteers—myself included. One night I'm pretty sure she phoned in crying and needing help. I didn't want to call her out since it's supposed to be anonymous, but I told her about the home that helped women get on their feet." Her eyes flooded with tears. "My mom…my dad…" She heaved a breath. "It was ugly growing up. When Vickie opened the home and hotline, I jumped in with both feet. I wish I could have done more for Lisa."

Mae understood. She'd suspected that life had been rough for Lilith in high school but she didn't know the exact stint. Like Mae, Lilith knew how to hide pain.

"What about boyfriends? Male friends? Wayne Furlow to be more specific."

Lilith rolled her eyes. "Wayne Furlow is a hound and a half and gets away with it because he's an expert at what he does. I saw him and Lisa walking to lunch together but the square is small and everybody knows everyone, however, he did have his hand on her lower back in a more than friendly way. And I hate to say this because it makes me sick—but that's just Wayne. Doesn't make it right. Doesn't make it an unwilling advance. But you know. Some men get away with it because of who they are. However, I've never heard any rumors about unwanted advances with Wayne. All consensual."

Mae understood the type. Flirtatious but harmless. Still. "You think Troy did it, don't you?"

"You don't?" She splayed her hands, palms out.

"Look, I like Cash. He's a nice guy, nowadays. And he never hurt women. But Troy isn't Cash. Cash feels like he has something to prove and by helping Troy it will make whatever happened to them growing up or between them better."

While Mae believed that someone was coming after them—she wasn't sure it had to do with who murdered Troy but someone who wanted the case halted because it would expose something else. "Well, I guess it can't hurt to investigate. If he did it then it will confirm Troy's guilt and that Cash can't save him. And if by some chance he is innocent then we have a real killer to catch who's getting off scot-free."

Lilith sighed. "I just hate that you're wasting your time when there are real cold cases with killers running free. If you need anything else, let me know. Vickie will be in her chambers by eight tomorrow morning if you want to catch her before court begins at nine."

"Will do. Let's have lunch tomorrow. You good?"

"Yeah. Probably be around one." They shared each other's contacts and Mae caught up with Cash coming out of Joe Sharp's chambers. He introduced them.

The chancellor was large and in charge. He was more salt than pepper and his hooded dark eyes made her squirm. "I was telling Detective Ryland that Lisa was a wonderful court reporter. She was well-liked and on the quiet side. I wish I knew more."

So did Mae.

When she and Cash reached the car they traded information as they drove back to the station, except for the fact that Lilith believed Troy was guilty. No point in tossing that out.

"What happened during divorce court? Lilith told me it got ugly." Cash hadn't mentioned that.

"Troy was distraught. He showed up half-drunk and angry. Lisa wanted the boat and Troy lost his cool. He came over the table and hollered about her taking everything from him. Judge Sharp held him in contempt. He did twenty-four hours in jail and Lisa got the boat."

Mae refrained from commenting on Troy's behavior. "After she died, what happened to the boat?"

"Troy took it, but he can't do anything with it. He's in prison. You don't think Troy beat Lisa to death over a boat, do you?"

"He beat her for no reasons at all, Cash. So yeah, maybe." At the SO parking lot, he pulled up beside her car.

"He didn't do it."

"Let's meet at chancery court in the morning at eight. Talk to Chancellor Vickie Pendergrass." She exited his vehicle, closed the door and climbed into her unbearably hot car. By the time she got to her childhood home, it was finally cooling off inside, but she was sticky and miserable.

She went in through the door to the kitchen. Mom had set the table and Dad and Barrett were already in their places while her mother brought platters and serving bowls to the table.

"Hi, honey. You hungry?" Mom asked.

"I could eat." She walked to the sink and washed her hands. "Let me help you."

"You believe that Ryland boy is innocent, Mae?" Dad asked. "Barrett says he did it."

Oh, well if Barrett said it then it must be true. She spooned green beans into a white serving bowl with little blue hearts around the edge. "I can't say for sure yet. But someone wants this case blocked from going any further."

"So you're going to keep purposely walking into danger? Seems pretty stupid to me," Dad said.

Mae placed the beans on the table with more force than necessary. "That's the job."

"A man's job, Mae. Let that other Ryland boy run headlong into danger. He can handle it." Dad's pursed lips were hidden by his bushy gray mustache and beard, but she'd seen the same look a hundred times over. His dark eyes held Mae's but unlike her mother, she refused to avert her gaze first.

She mentally counted to ten.

"Women got no business in truck stops and over the road alone or in other dangerous jobs. They could get hurt."

"By men. If men would keep their eyes and paws to themselves, it wouldn't be dangerous for women. So instead of telling them to stay home or in 'safe' jobs, how about telling men to stop being such slimeballs and learn how to treat women with respect!"

Dad's thick eyebrow rose, but his voice stayed cool and calm. "Men are gonna be men, Mae. Ain't no changing."

"I'll give you that." She looked at Mom who sat with her head down and hands in her lap. Not coming to Mae's defense or agreeing with her. She never had. Not now and not then. When Davie Deerborn knocked her down on the playground and she came home and told, Dad said it was because he liked her. Mom said to avoid him. When Landon Murry lied and humiliated her, the coach and her father said, *boys will be boys* and nothing was done. When she punched him after overhearing his lewd and crass talk about her, Dad told her she'd never land a man by being so dominant. She got detention. Landon got away with it all.

Mom said zip. Did zip.

Nothing had ever gone Mae's way. Dad had never come to her rescue or aid or told her that she could run as fast or faster than boys or even be her own person. Mom never defended her. Never told her once that she could be anything she wanted to be. It was unspoken but expected to get married, have babies and raise a family—and nothing more unless she wanted to be a teacher or secretary or have some other safe "woman's job." Well, it wasn't the fifties anymore.

"I'm going to Grandma Rose's. She needs someone looking out for her anyway." She rushed from the kitchen, threw her bags together and blew out of the house.

Barrett followed her. "Dad is Dad, Mae. You know this. You having PMS?"

She rammed her last bag in the back seat and gritted her teeth. "No, Barrett, I am not having PMS. I am having the last straw." She slammed the door and spun on him. "You're exactly like him."

Barrett narrowed his eyes. "I am not. But he has a point. He's trying to protect you."

"I don't want protected—I want approval." Well, she might have wanted some protection like when she'd been slandered. She slid into the driver's seat. "I want to be who I am, not who he thinks I ought to be."

"Mae," Barrett pleaded. "Stay. He loves you and he's just old-fashioned and set in his ways."

"No, he's a male chauvinist and I'm over it." She peeled out of the drive and sped to Grandma Rose's.

She parked in the drive and pounded on the door. "Grandma Rose!" She was hard of hearing these days. Mae rounded the side of the house and knelt at the fake rock that held the spare house key. Such a dangerous thing. The key was missing.

She grumbled under her breath and headed to the back of the house. "Grandma Rose!" She banged on the door then peered into the kitchen window beside it and gasped. "Grandma Rose!"

Mae used her gun and broke out the window, moved the glass with the bottom of her shirt and climbed inside. Grandma Rose was unconscious on the kitchen floor.

A trickle of blood ran down her temple.

FIVE

Mae slid to the floor next to Grandma Rose and felt for a pulse. *Oh, thank You, Jesus!* She whipped out her cell phone and called for an ambulance. Mae scanned the room as she held Grandma Rose's hand. It appeared she'd fallen in the kitchen and struck her head on the edge of the table, which was smudged with blood. How long had she been lying unconscious? Mae should have stayed here all along. Mom should have pushed the issue about Grandma Rose moving in with them or going to assisted living. But Grandma was as genteel as a Southern belle could be, and everyone knew belles were headstrong and not to be trifled with.

The sirens wailed in the distance and within seconds paramedics were rushing in the door and lifting Grandma's frail body onto a gurney and hooking her up to monitors. Mae followed behind them in her car and called Mom to update her. She parked on the farthest lot from the ER department and rushed inside as the hospital staff hurried Grandma Rose back.

God, please let her be okay.

Grandma Rose had always been her source of comfort and her cheerleading squad. She couldn't lose her. Mae sat in a coral chair and bobbed her knee, waiting and hoping everything would be fine. She texted her team members in their group chat to ask them to pray for Grandma Rose and let them know she'd keep them posted. She also updated them on Troy's case. She wasn't ruling out Wayne Furlow as a suspect. She'd seen too many people on the right side of the law do wrong things.

To calm her nerves, Mae used her phone to pull up Lisa Ryland's social media sites. Instagram was mostly selfies with inspirational quotes attached, which Mae found to be nothing short of vanity masked as inspiration. Lisa wasn't fooling anyone. She might as well have captioned them all "Hey, look at me!" which revealed insecurity and the need for attention and approval. Mae could relate to needing approval, but instead of traveling through one toxic relationship after another, Mae had avoided relationships altogether. The hurt wasn't worth it. Lisa, like many victims, entered cycles of abusive men. Same man, different name. Did she find someone who went further than Troy? If Lisa was in the talks of going back to Troy, then maybe a man she was seeing didn't like that. Didn't want Troy to have her back. When he couldn't get what he wanted, he took matters into his own hands. Mae had seen it time and again. Possibly one of the men she had taken photos with in her Instagram. There were two. A few months apart and not long after her divorce. They didn't appear romantic in nature but that meant nothing.

The sliding doors opened. Dad, Barrett and Mom hurried to her side.

"Any news?" Dad asked.

"No. She's been back there for almost twenty minutes. I've just been sitting here working a man's job, and waiting."

He ignored her jab and she told them what she suspected happened. Mom sank in a chair and held her head in her hands. Dad laid a steady hand on her shoulder, and Mom reached for it, squeezing. Not that Mae hadn't ever seen her father display affection for Mom, but it wasn't often.

Barrett peeked at her phone from over her shoulder. "What are you working on?"

"You know what I'm working on. Lisa Ryland's case. You hear of any talk about her seeing anyone after or even before her divorce from Troy?"

Barrett frowned. "Why would I have?"

Mae gave him the duh face. "Because you worked at the courthouse with her. It's not a big place with a lot of people."

"Well, I didn't," he shot off hard and fast. He shoved his hands into his pockets. "It's a lost cause, Mae. Troy killed her. Cash is chasing wind and he has you running after it too."

"I'm not so sure."

Barrett snorted. "You're all lusty-dusted like every other woman in town over Cash. If he tells you the boogeyman killed her you'd believe it."

Mae's ire rose. "I'm not anything with Cash. And I didn't believe it at first but after his stabbing, Troy's attack and our near-death experiences, I'm inclined to believe that something sinister is in play. Maybe it's not the killer. It could be that Troy did kill Lisa. But it's someone who is fast becoming a killer to hide something they don't want found with a new investigation."

Barrett rolled his eyes. "If it's all work why were you with him so late at night then?"

"I was working."

"Can't do that at the SO?" He raised his eyebrows. "Whatever. What you do is your business. But you're barking up the wrong tree." He plopped in a chair near the TV and took great interest in the news. In an hour, the doctor greeted them.

"Rose had a stroke that caused her to fall. We've moved her to the ICU. She's had some decline in mental status. We'll monitor her and do further testing. One visitor at a time."

Dad asked a few questions and then the doctor left them. At the elevator, her stomach roiled but the last thing she needed was Dad and Barrett giving her a hard time for hating enclosed, small spaces. She stepped in and hummed inside her head until the door opened to the second floor. Mae exited first and let out a quiet but relieved breath.

"Debbie," Dad said, "why don't you go on in and see her first. Come get me if you need me."

Mom nodded and disappeared down the hall.

A nurse came around the corner and caught Mae's eye. Average height, slight frame, honey blond hair pulled back in a ponytail and dark circles under her bright green eyes. Mae would recognize her high school friend and college roommate—for the first year—anywhere.

Mae approached the nurses' station. "Lauren?" she said softly. She hadn't seen her since the summer after Mae graduated and informed Lauren that she was joining the police academy and that she was the reason why. Mae had taken enough harassment but when Lauren was drugged at a college party and taken advantage of—and nothing was done on her behalf—Mae decided someone needed to fight for women's justice. And if no one was going to, then Mae would. She'd make sure they were heard and helped.

Lauren smiled then grabbed Mae in a monster hug. "Mae! I'd say it's good to see you but if you're on this floor…"

"My grandmother had a stroke. She was just put in a room—212."

"I'll be her night nurse. Grandma Rose?"

"Yes."

She patted Mae's shoulder in sympathy. "I'm sorry. I'll take excellent care of her."

"Lauren," said a nurse with tight curls, pointing to the station, "you got another bouquet, girl. Mmph…" She shook her head and breezed past them.

A huge vase of pink roses brightened up the fluorescent halls.

Lauren sighed.

"Anniversary?"

Lauren's laugh was humorless. "I got married four years ago. Divorced two years ago. It was…another bad choice on my part. Guess I got what I deserved… again," she said with resentment and regret.

Mae's protectiveness kicked in. "Lauren, you did not deserve what happened to you by that idiot frat boy and whatever ensued with your husband was not deserved. I'm sure." She'd hoped Lauren would have found the strength to believe that regardless of what she wore that night or how much she drank, it did in no way mean she deserved someone to viciously assault her. Lauren hadn't been able to go on and dropped out in the middle of second semester. And the rich frat boy who did it had lawyers who'd intimidated Lauren and made her believe a jury would see her as asking for it. She'd refused to press charges no matter how hard her parents and Mae had begged her to. He went on to graduate and go to med school with zero repercussions.

"I know. I guess sometimes I can't drag myself out of the dark place. But I'm such a pitiful person dumping on you after seeing you for one second in almost ten years. The flowers are from a guy I dated a few times but we broke up and this is his way of trying to make it work. I'm just not ready, you know? But I guess it's sweet—the pursuit."

Mae didn't see it that way. Red flags were flying. "You can dump on me anytime. And if he won't take a hint, you can call the sheriff's office and file a complaint. Pursuit after a denial feels more like stalking."

Lauren chewed on her thumbnail. "True. I don't know. He's not being pushy. Just leaving little gifts... and he *is* a deputy. Anyway, he's harmless. Are you home for your grandma?"

"Yes, but that was before the stroke. Now I'm on a case." She told her why she was here.

"Wow, working with Cash. I can't believe teachers actually thought that paper was his. It was obvious he didn't write it. I hated that you lost out on the valedictorian spot. You deserved it. I guess we both lost in some areas." She checked her watch. "Hey, let's catch up. Have breakfast? No depressing talk. My shift ends at 7:00 a.m. I'm usually starving. Wanna meet at 7:15 at Hank's tomorrow?"

Hank's wasn't far from chancery court. "It'll be kinda short. I have to be at the courthouse at eight, but I'm game if that's okay."

Lauren's eyes lit up. "Sounds great." They traded numbers. "Text me if anything changes."

"Thanks, and if you need anything at all, please don't hesitate to call or text me." She hugged her. "I feel so much better knowing that you're going to be taking care of Grandma Rose." She caught her mom coming into the waiting area. "How is she?" she asked Mom as Dad and Barrett approached.

"Sleeping but she's so pale. I'm going to stay the night out here in a recliner but y'all go on home and get some sleep. I'll be back in time to pack your lunch, Dale."

"Call if you need anything." He kissed her forehead. "I will."

Barrett kissed Mom's cheek. "Call if you need me."

Mae followed Dad and Barrett to the doors. "Hey, Barrett, do you know which deputy Lauren Jenkins was seeing?" Did Lauren even go by her maiden name? She had no idea who she'd married and divorced.

"Was? I didn't know she and Billy broke up. He never mentioned it."

"Billy Anderson?" The deputy who'd shown up at Cash's last night?

"Yeah. Why?"

"No reason. See you tomorrow, I guess." She watched him jog to his marked unit and zoom out of the parking lot. The sun had dipped behind the horizon an hour ago. The heat hadn't let up much, though. Mae was exhausted but didn't want Mom to sit alone. She kept her company until nearly midnight when Mom all but pushed her out the door.

Mae rubbed her aching neck as she strode through the dimly lit parking lot to her car. Hairs on her neck rose and she paused, scanning the lot. The feel of lurking eyes on her sent a shiver down her spine. Nothing but shadows and the flashing lights of the ambulance parked under the ER awning.

She retrieved her keys and cautiously strode toward her Jetta. When she approached the driver's side, she noticed the back tire was flat. Mae groaned and pinched the bridge of her nose. Cash's tires had been slashed. Had these? It was dark and hard to tell the cause of the flat. As she bent to inspect the damage, something hard cracked against her back, knocking the breath from her.

She landed on her stomach, but rolled over to see a masked, dark figure towering over her. Mae raised her hands to block the next blow of the baseball bat. She grabbed it as it came down and yanked it over her head, throwing her attacker off-balance. He dropped the weapon.

Mae jumped to her feet and hollered for help, hoping to grab the attention of the paramedics sitting outside their ambulance. The attacker was light on his feet and swung a meaty, gloved fist but Mae jerked backward and took a clip to the edge of her chin. Not enough to knock her down or out but enough to rattle her teeth.

She could run or fight. Mae was no runner.

She threw a punch but her arm wasn't long enough to connect. The attacker rushed her and brought out a switchblade.

This changed the game.

Mae had left her gun on the kitchen floor at Grandma Rose's. If she could get the bat and knock the blade from his grip, she might have a chance to even the score and win a point or two.

Headlights revealed a truck entering the lot; they

shone right on Mae and her attacker, then a horn blared. The black-clad figure bolted, scrambling over a car hood and disappearing down a row of parked vehicles. Mae turned and the lights dimmed.

Cash jumped out of the truck—the assailant already hopping in a dark colored truck and blasting from the lot—and pointed to the bat. "Little midnight baseball going on?" His tone was teasing but the worry and concern in his eyes were hard to miss as he tried to appear nonchalant in his inspection for physical wounds.

"I'm fine. And ha. Ha." Mae let out a heavy breath. "You have impeccable timing."

"You sure you're all right?"

She nodded.

He peered into the dark parking lot. "I was working late at the station. Troy's case isn't the only one I'm working on. With only three of us, we basically investigate every homicide together. Doesn't really matter who is actually the lead detective on the case. Barrett filled me in. Said you were probably still at the hospital. I brought you and your mama some good coffee."

If she weren't still mad at him for being a pain in high school, she'd have kissed him and maybe proposed on the spot. He'd saved her bacon and brought her caffeine.

After serving Mae's mom a cup of coffee—and not telling her Mae had been attacked in the parking lot—Cash had watched Mae change her slashed tire because she refused to allow him to do it for her. He'd felt like a heel standing over her as she removed the flat and replaced it with the spare without hesitation. Naturally, she would be able to change tires. There wasn't anything she couldn't do. She'd been in a fighting stance when he'd whipped into the parking lot. It had been only a flash before the attacker ran away but Mae was going to fight that guy and he'd had a knife. Cash wasn't sure if she was brilliant or bullheaded—or maybe both.

He parked behind her in her grandma's drive. She'd told him about how she'd found her. She hadn't explained why she'd decided to stay here instead of at her parents' home and he hadn't asked.

"Hey, thanks for following me home. I appreciate it. You've done more than you needed to."

Cash shrugged. "You gonna fix that window you said you broke?"

Mae groaned. "Yes. I forgot after being attacked."

"I can do it right quick. No big deal. I have some tools and probably some plywood in the bed of my truck from a project I was working on. It's kind of late."

Mae snorted. "Kinda? It's nearly 1:30 in the morning. I'd tell you I can do it, but I'm beat. Although, you have stitches and a bum leg."

He grinned. "True. I'll just leave you to it then." Her face fell and he laughed. "I'm kidding. I'm fine." He pulled his toolbox from his truck and the smallest piece of plywood he could find. "I built a custom doghouse for the Rollins family. Had some leftover scraps I hadn't tossed yet. Good thing."

"Yeah," Mae said as she led him around back, "you never know when you need to board up a window that's been broken into."

He held up his cell phone, using the flashlight to inspect the window she'd smashed out. "Not a bad job."

"Guess you'd know." She grinned then held up a

hand. "Sorry. I wasn't being snarky about your past. I was teasing."

No hard feelings taken. He heard the innocence in her tone. "No worries. If you could turn on the kitchen and the back-porch lights, that would help me."

When he had enough light, he went to work boarding up the window. "I know a guy. I can call him to replace this tomorrow."

"Thanks," she called then came outside beside him. "You get caught up on other cases you're working?"

Between his hammering and pounding, he hoped he didn't wake and irk neighbors. "Yeah. Reports mostly." He'd recorded his notes and passed them off to Teri to type but stuck around while she did it. It wasn't like he was gonna chill while she offered to do extra work on his behalf. Not that he hadn't initially done the work, but recording the information was faster and easier— to him.

"I hate paperwork."

"Me too. I'd rather be doing anything else." He hammered in the last nail.

"Like boarding up windows in the wee hours of the morning?" Humor laced her voice. He was enjoying the easy banter between them. It had been like this before the stolen essay. After Mae had warmed up to him. She'd been standoffish like a timid dog for the first few weeks she'd tutored him.

"Something like that." He'd rather be hammering nails into his own head than doing paperwork. He finished and brushed his hands on his jeans then collected his tools. "I don't feel right leaving you alone, though I know you can take care of yourself."

"Exactly. I can. I have a gun and I know how to use

it. Go get some sleep—8:00 is coming early for us. And I have a breakfast appointment." She paused. "What do you know about Chancellor Pendergrass's Domestic Crisis Hotline and safe house?"

"Not much. They don't give out the address to just anyone to protect domestic violence victims. I know Judge Pendergrass holds a big fancy party every July and it involves a silent auction to raise funds for the house and the needs of the women. Everyone in law enforcement, the political scene and big business is invited. The sheriff encourages us to attend. Black tie and all." Wasn't his thing. Hobnobbing and drinking flutes of champagne, but he believed in the cause.

"You don't like going?"

"I give monastery gifts but I don't love wearing a penguin suit."

Mae grinned and handed him his toolbox. "You need sleep. It's *monetary* gift, not *monastery*—unless you're a monk." She chuckled and he took the toolbox, feeling like a tool himself.

"Well, it's late."

"Yes, it is."

"See ya bright and early. Enjoy your breakfast." Had she taken Way Becker up on his offer? A streak of green pumped irritation through his blood.

"I will. By the way, I'm having breakfast with a friend in the morning. Lauren Jenkins. What do you know about her dating Billy Anderson? She said she broke up with him but he's been sending her flowers and little gifts to her work. Can't seem to take the hint. Is he pushy?"

Relief that her breakfast was with a woman washed

over him. "He's got a lot of bravado but I don't think he's one to overstep. Did she say he was?"

"Not in so many words, but no means no. She's already been through the wringer. The last thing she needs is another man not taking no for an answer."

Cash nodded. "I'll look into it."

"Thank you."

He waved and strode to his truck, his side protesting his carpentry job. By the time he got home and got some sleep it was about time to get up. He awoke with dry, itchy eyes and a serious need for caffeine. At 8:00 a.m., Mae breezed through the front doors of the chancery court, showing her badge to the officers on security duty. She met him with a cheery smile, but faint dark circles under her eyes revealed the need for more rest. He could relate. "How was breakfast?"

"Sunny-side up." She held up a paper sack. "I had a feeling you might not have eaten anything so I brought a muffin. Chocolate chip."

The gesture threw him for a small loop. Not only that he might be hungry—and he was—but that she remembered how much he liked the chocolate-chip muffins from Hank's. They'd tutored there on several occasions and Hank served that baked good all day until they were gone.

"Thank you. I appreciate it. I've only had coffee." He accepted the bag and the scent of chocolate and a hint of cinnamon reminded him of his hunger. His stomach growled and he bit into the oversize muffin. "I haven't had one of these in a while."

Mae shrugged. "I'm a big believer in breakfast. For any meal." They strolled down the halls leading to the judge's chambers. The courthouse was quiet with only a few people and hushed voices.

Cash knocked on Judge Pendergrass's chamber door. Lilith opened it and smiled. "Morning."

"Morning," Cash said.

"We still on for lunch?" Lilith asked Mae.

"Far as I know. If things get wonky, I'll text you. I had breakfast with Lauren Jenkins this morning."

"I haven't seen her in a few months. How is she?" Lilith asked.

"She's hanging in. Went back to her maiden name after her divorce."

Lilith's eyes radiated pity. "Chancellor Pendergrass presided over her divorce. I assume she told you a bit about that."

"She did." They exchanged a knowing glance but said no more. Must have been domestic violence. "Can we speak with Chancellor Pendergrass?"

"I told her y'all were coming this morning." Lilith led them into the chancellor's inner chambers. Chancellor Pendergrass sat in her judge's robe behind an ornate pine desk. Her hair was long and wavy and silvery brown. She didn't look like a woman in her late fifties. She cast her brown eyes, which had likely had some cosmetic work, on them and smiled with collagen-injected lips. She stood and extended her hand. Firm. Strong. "Detective Ryland, good to see you." She shook Mae's hand. "Agent Vogel, nice to meet you. Lilith speaks highly of you."

"It's nice to meet you," Mae said.

"Please have a seat." Judge Pendergrass returned to her cushy leather chair and Cash and Mae perched in the matching light gray wingback chairs on the other side of her desk. "Lilith tells me you've reopened Mr. Ryland's case."

Cash exchanged glances with Mae and gave her a subtle nod. Judge Pendergrass might be more apt to talk with another woman with more candidness than the man who wanted his abusive brother out of prison.

"What can you tell us about Lisa?" Mae asked.

Vickie leaned forward on her desk, tenting her fingers. "Lisa was sweet. But she was lonely and insecure. Quiet until she trusted you." She glanced at Cash. "I'm sorry if this hurts your feelings, but Troy's abuse and their fights that didn't end in physical violence as well as the ones that did took their toll on her. She became withdrawn toward the end. I recognized the signs and talked to Lisa about the abuse and the stress at home."

"And what did she say?" Mae asked.

Cash's gut roiled and the muffin he'd just eaten wanted to come up. He felt responsible and Judge Pendergrass's eagle eye all but screamed he might as well be a wifebeater too.

"She wanted out but she loved him. He didn't mean it but when he was drunk he changed. When he was sober he could be loving and attentive. He'd buy her gifts. Much of what we hear in domestic abuse cases. His gifts were apologies. We talked about all that and the fact that it would repeat. She left him for a time."

"About three months," Cash offered.

Judge Pendergrass arched an eyebrow. "She told me you put a deposit down for her on a little rental house two miles from you. How kind." Her tone didn't imply he'd been kind or that he'd done enough. If she was going to leave Troy, Cash thought being close to him would be safer. Guess not.

Mae cleared her throat and redirected the judge's attention. "Why did she go back?"

"Why do most women?" Lilith said. "They love them. Their husbands sweet-talk them. My dad did that to my mom dozens of times. Not to mention he was a stable financial provider. But Lisa made a nice living and knew that."

Judge Pendergrass agreed.

"During those few months, did you notice any changes in her behavior? Another man—even just a friend?"

"She had some light come back to her eyes," the chancellor said. "I imagine she gained some breathing room. I saw her at lunch once with the district attorney. It didn't appear to be romantic, though. I never asked her about it." She looked at Lilith, who stood near the door that led to the courtroom and her bench. "Did you?"

Lilith shook her head. "I'm sure they were friends and we all know Wayne. But I don't believe it went any further. And then she went back to Troy. Lisa wasn't the cheating type."

Not everyone was a cheating type but that didn't mean they didn't cheat. If Wayne wanted more from Lisa and she went back to Troy he could have been angry enough to kill her. Cash couldn't see it but love and hate had a fine line between them and many times it was a motive for murder.

"Anyone at all who might have had a beef with her?" Mae questioned.

The chancellor tapped her chin with dark red nails. "You know I can't say a beef, per se, but I do remember once we were having lunch at Windy City Grille—most attorneys and court employees eat there—and she noted that one of the defense attorneys creeped her out. She excused herself to the restroom while he collected his to-go order. I'd never seen them together, though."

"Name?" Mae asked and put her pen to the paper.

"Harrison Trout. Defense attorney. Detective Ryland, you may be familiar with him."

He was more than familiar with Troy's defense attorney.

SIX

"Who was Lisa's closest girlfriend?" Mae asked. "If Harrison Trout had given Lisa a reason for the creeps, a girlfriend would know."

Cash sat at the table in one of the rooms they used to interview suspects but the sheriff had allowed them to turn it into a space to work the cold case. He massaged the back of his neck. "She ran around with Holly Prewett. They were friends in high school and kept up with one another. She was with her during divorce court. And she testified against Troy. Naturally, she's avoided me."

"We need to talk to her. Can you get her number? I'll see what I can come up with on Harrison Trout. Any rumors or anything?"

Cash threw his paper cup of coffee into the trash can by the door. "Single. Late thirties. Meathead. Works out at the Edge Fitness center. I've seen him there a few times. He moved here about five years ago from the Gulf Coast. Louisiana maybe. I can't remember. His office is next door to Fitz Leeman's office. Fitz was Lisa's divorce attorney."

"I'd like to talk to him too. In person."

Cash understood. Phone interviews were convenient

and they did them often, but it wasn't the same as seeing a person's face and studying their body language.

"What do we know about Fitz Leeman?"

"Not much. He's married and has a couple kids. Mid-forties. He didn't play around. Lisa got almost everything."

"Including the boat."

Including that. Cash preferred interviews and hands-on digging. He wasn't good at research on the computer. He used Siri often to search for him and he had color-coded software he used on his laptop to help him read the letters. A deep navy blue font on a softer cream—not white—background. He also had audio software that would read files to him, thanks to Charlie, his mentor, who had aided him in connecting with some experts in Memphis who had provided the tools needed to make his life and job less complicated. The sheriff had made allowances for him and he'd always appreciate that.

But with Mae sitting right in front of him, he didn't want to work with speech-to-text software or have her see his special fonts and color-coding systems.

"You gonna get to work anytime soon?" Mae asked.

His gut knotted. "Just thinking." He stood. "I need coffee to make my brain work. Want some?"

"Sure." She clacked on her laptop, engaged and moving swiftly. He envied and admired that. He hurried to the coffeepot and used his speech-to-text to have Teri quickly meet up with him.

She hobbled over—she'd been in a skiing incident on vacation two weeks ago and was on light duty. She hated it. "What's up, Cash?"

Heat rose in his cheeks. "I need some information and I don't want to use my speech software or—"

"Or reveal to the pretty blonde you do things differently. Cash, you're a great detective. There's no shame in your accommodations." She blew an unruly brunette bang from her eye and sighed. "What do you need? I could use a break from filing anyway. See if I ski again anytime soon. This stinks."

Cash knew Teri was right but it didn't make a dent in the shame or measure of fear. Mae had called him smart twice. He'd like her to keep that view. "Fitz Leeman. Get me what you can on him and cross-reference him with Lisa."

"You think the divorce attorney might have done it?"

"I don't know jack at this point. I only know it wasn't Troy." Cash had called early this morning to check in on him. He was still in the prison infirmary and recovering well. He had extra guards on him. That brought some relief but not enough. "Also, I need more information on Tommy Leonard, who may have stabbed Troy. His defense attorney was Harrison Trout—same as Troy. We have a witness that states Lisa got the creeps from Trout and hid in the bathroom one day at lunch. If you can chase down any of that it would be helpful. Text me if you get anything and I'll meet you back here."

Teri chuckled and shook her head. "Since when has truth been a covert mission?" She saluted and he poured two coffees, remembering Mae drank hers black. His side was tender and his leg throbbed but he wasn't so bad off he needed light duty.

He gave Mae her cup and eased into his office chair, bringing up his laptop and turning it where she couldn't see. "I'm going to dig into Fitz Leeman."

Mae's eyes grew wide. "Maybe pause on that a sec. I think I have something worth looking into."

Cash leaned over. "What?"

"Did some searching on Harrison Trout back in Louisiana and found that he had a restraining order against him by a Tamera Smith. For stalking. It never went anywhere but about eight months later, he transferred here. What if that's why Lisa got the heebie-jeebies over him? Could he have been stalking her? I just ran another local search. No restraining orders or formal charges brought but there have been two complaints in the last three years on Harrison Trout for harassment and stalking. Kelly Wetzell and Marianne Scott. Midthirties. Blonde. One single and one divorced." She clacked away on the keyboard. "Marianne Scott used Fitz Leeman as her divorce attorney. You said he's next door to Harrison, right?"

"Yeah." A sinking feeling in Cash's gut told him they were onto something ugly. If he had been stalking Lisa, he could have easily killed her when she refused his advances, and being Troy's attorney only sweetened the deal for him. "Have any of the women been assaulted or attacked?"

"I don't know. No charges." Mae's nostrils flared. "Once again...women being terrorized and too afraid to act and the violator walking away with nothing but a slap on the wrist if that. But the truth is when it comes to stalking laws they're weak."

"Let's call the woman in Louisiana and get her story then talk to the local women personally," Cash offered.

"You want to do the interview or keep digging on Trout?"

"I'll take Tamera Smith. Lisa was my sister-in-law so that might give me an edge."

"Valid." She rattled off the number and he memorized it then punched in the digits. It rang twice before a woman with a Cajun accent answered.

"Ms. Smith, this is Detective Cash Ryland with the Criminal Investigation Division in Willow Banks, Mississippi. I'd like to talk to you about a man named Harrison Trout."

Mae's stomach rumbled reminding her that she'd had to cancel lunch with Lilith. Mae had texted her over an hour ago with apologies but Lilith understood the job and what was at stake. The day was going to be chock-full and she'd be shocked if she had the chance for a bite before dinner.

She'd called Mom to check on Grandma Rose. She was in and out, didn't seem too alert but her vitals were stable. She had some mobility loss on her left side but the doctor said it might return. Too early to tell.

Mae scrolled through her emails on her phone as Cash turned onto Spring Valley Drive toward Jenner Elevator to speak with Marianne Scott. His earlier phone call to Tamera Smith had been interesting. Tamera had met Harrison Trout when she'd accompanied her sister to a court hearing that had nothing to do with him. But he'd introduced himself and they chatted. Tamera was single. Not necessarily looking, but he'd been attractive and charming. She went to one dinner. It hadn't been a romantic connection on her part. According to Tamera, Harrison had been too flaunting about his career and money.

She'd declined another date. But he'd pushed, pressed and all but staked out her house. She had a restraining order put on him. He'd found ways around it but her brother had shown up one night and caught him sitting outside her house. Messed him up and after that Harrison moved.

Cash had called Lisa's best friend. According to Holly, Lisa hadn't said she'd been stalked but she got a bad vibe from him—she'd catch him staring at her when she worked in district court. Lisa was glad to be in chancery court but never said Harrison was the reason for her transfer.

But it could have been. In Mae's experience, women often remained quiet about harassment due to fear of being called out or chastised or for the thoughts that it was harmless and they could handle it. It didn't always turn out for the best.

"I'm not sure popping in on Marianne Scott is smart, Cash. She might need time to mentally prepare if Harrison terrorized her. The memories will be overwhelming." Cash parked at the front. Perhaps maybe a dozen vehicles in the huge parking lot. "Plus, this place is huge and practically empty since it's being dissolved and going out of business. Scary memories might make her paranoid here alone."

Cash turned off the engine. "I understand. But something else I know is people want to put bad experiences out of mind. They bury them in deep vaults and lock them away. If we called her first she'd have it locked up tight. We need to hear everything. I won't badger her or press her to the point of no return. Trust me."

Mac should have locked up her doubtful thoughts. Cash noted the skepticism in her eyes with a sigh.

"Bad choice of words. I know you don't trust me. But you can, Mae." His blue eyes met hers and held… as if he were willing her to trust and believe in him.

She wanted to if for no other reason than he'd saved her. Protected her.

"I'll follow your lead but if she gets into a panicked state, I'm calling it." It was the best she could do. Mae couldn't confess she would or could trust him fully. She didn't.

"Fair enough." He locked the doors to the unit and they strode inside the chilly building. The place was deserted. A young guy in his late twenties passed by.

"Can I help you?" He spotted Cash's badge clipped to his belt along with his gun then made a sweeping pass at Mae. She wore her badge and gun in the same way. His eyes widened.

"We're looking for Marianne Scott. Do you know where we can find her?"

He nodded with a blank look. "Third floor. End of the hall."

"Thank you," Cash said and walked to the elevators. He punched the up arrow and the doors opened. Mae paused.

Cash stepped one foot inside and frowned. "You want to take the stairs?"

"Yes, but it's only an elevator. I take them all the time. I just hate them." She entered and hummed inside her head. The doors opened to the third floor and relief flooded her as they ambled down the hall to Marianne Scott's office.

They knocked and startled the attractive blonde.

"Sorry. We didn't mean to scare you."

Marianne grinned and clutched her chest. "No, it's fine. I've gotten used to it being only me and one other employee up here. Second floor is empty and rarely does anyone on the ground level visit. Shannon is off today so it's just me," she nervously rambled.

"We apologize." Cash and Mae removed their badges from their belts then introduced themselves. Mae took the lead.

"We're here to ask you a few questions about Harrison Trout."

Her eyes went on alert. "What's he done?"

"Maybe nothing but we're looking into a case and it's possible he may have stalked the victim—could you share your story?"

Marianne shivered. "I met him—bumped into him really—when I was meeting with my divorce attorney, Fitz Leeman. Their offices are next to one another. He was nice, charming, attractive. We chitchatted a couple of times and I did give him my number, but when he asked me to dinner, I realized I was a mess and not ready, plus my divorce wasn't final. I politely declined and was honest with him. He sent me flowers at work, candy, some texts. Eventually he showed up at my home. I filed a complaint. It's been several months since I've heard from him but I'm wary all the time."

"Understandable." After she filed a complaint, he focused on Kelly Wetzell. Lisa could have been victimized and who knew how many after her that never reported him. Stalkers typically escalated. Harrison seemed to fixate on someone new when threatened. He was smart enough to know that he could lose his practice and even his license depending on how far he took it. "Anything else you could tell us? Did you know Lisa Ryland?"

"No, but I remember hearing about her murder on

the news. I thought her ex-husband did it. I saw Harrison was his defense attorney."

They didn't have any further questions. Her story was much like the woman Cash had called from Louisiana and Kelly's would no doubt be similar, as well. They left her office and headed for the elevator. Cash paused.

"You want to take the stairs?" he said again.

"I'm fine. It's only a few seconds. What do you make of this stalker angle?"

Cash pushed the button on the elevator. "I think he could easily have framed Troy. He knows the law, forensics... I like him for it more than I do Wayne Furlow. Trout might not want us digging because we'll discover he did indeed stalk Lisa. Also, he has access to the guy who tried to kill my brother. He could have lured him to do it with ways to appeal his case. Who knows."

The door opened and they stepped inside. Mae began comfort humming in her head.

"We need to find someone who could help us know if Harrison actually—"

Thud!

The elevator bounced then froze; the interior lights went out. Mae's heart lurched into her throat. "Uh— Cash?"

Cash frowned, switched on his cell phone flashlight and pushed the button that opened the elevator.

Nothing.

Mae's heart rate spiked, and perspiration broke out on her forehead and upper lip. Her insides felt fevered. "Are we stuck?"

He muttered under his breath and mashed a few more buttons then pressed the help button. He waited. Nothing.

"What are we going to do?" she asked, hearing the panic in her voice.

Cash studied her then laid his hands on her shoulders. "Elevators get jammed from time to time. I'm sure we're fine. I need you to breathe deep and stand up straight to calm your heart rate. Panicking only messes with oxygen levels. Can you do that?"

She nodded, unsure if she could or not but she'd try.

Cash pressed the help button and called out, banging on the door. "Hello! Anyone?"

The building was sparse. If they were in between floors Marianne or anyone else wouldn't be able to hear well.

"Sometimes, you need to press your floor number again." Cash tried but to no avail and it sent Mae right back to borderline hysteria. She banged on the stainless-steel door with her fists and hollered, then turned with her back flush against the doors.

"I can't believe this is happening." She ripped off a shoe and used that to bang on the door but it was dead silent. "What if a cable loosens and we fall?"

"That rarely happens. Mostly in movies. Focus on something. Tell me about an interesting cold case you worked on." He studied his cell phone and frowned. "No reception." He mumbled under his breath. "Cold case. Go."

Mae thought. "Well, we worked on a case about a high school football star who was murdered."

"Oh yeah?" He banged and hollered for help. "You close the case?"

"We did." Talking about that case helped but not enough to keep her from feeling like she might faint at any moment. "Cash, I don't know how much more of this I can take. What are the chances an elevator in an elevator company would stick like this?"

Cash sighed. "Slim. It's possible we were followed by the killer. It wouldn't take a rocket scientist to figure out how to mess with the control panel or the breaker to shut down the power. He could have done it while we were talking with Marianne. Or it's just a coincidence."

That did nothing for Mae's state of mind.

"Take my cell so I can use both hands to open the door and see where we are. We might be able to get onto another floor."

Mae took the cell while Cash worked to pry open the center doors. No go. He punched the wall and observed the top of the elevator and tried the help button again. Nothing.

"One more go," he said and worked his fingers through the door. Muscles in his neck and forehead popped and underneath his shirt, his biceps bulged. Slowly the door began to open until he had it ajar with his foot. "Looks like we're in between the third and second floors."

There was about a foot or two of space and then she could see the second-floor tile.

"I'm going to hold the door open while you shimmy out."

Cash would hold the door open for her but how would he get out without it cutting him in half? "I don't know that I like that idea. It leaves you vulnerable."

"While I appreciate your professional concern for me, Mae, it's our best and only option." Cash's tone carried authority without being arrogant. And he was right. She also noted his use of *professional* next to *concern*. But was it all professional?

It had certainly started that way, but the hours they'd spent together and his ability to come through for her and keep her protected had shifted the scales holding personal and professional. They weren't evenly balanced, but she had to admit that professionalism now weighed measurably lighter than personal.

If he were seriously injured it'd hit where it hurt— personally. Right in the heart. But she couldn't go there.

"Mae, I'm not out of shape but this is heavy." His legs were shaking. "Move on through."

"How will you escape?"

"I don't know. You can go get help."

"And leave you here alone? Not hardly. I'll get out and find something to hold these doors open long enough for you to get to safety too."

He nodded, sweat beading on his forehead.

She scrambled under his legs and through the opening to the second floor. "Hold still and I'll find something!" Gun in hand, she rushed down the hall searching in and out of offices—most of them empty until she found a walker in a storage closet. She carried it back. "It's metal and it's durable."

Cash's leg was involuntarily convulsing as he held the door open. Mae shoved the walker up and through the space between floors and Cash used his other foot to wedge it then released his leg and it held.

"I'm coming. Thanks." He slipped under the space when the walker shifted.

"Cash, move! Now!" Mac hollered.

Just as Cash slid through the space on the second floor the doors snapped shut with a loud thwack. He lay on the hall floor breathing heavily, his hands on his heaving chest.

Mae let out a relieved sigh and bent over. "You scared me half to death."

Cash let out a shaky laugh. "Scared myself. Let's get out of here."

"I'm not a huge believer in coincidences where murder is concerned."

"Neither am I."

"What if it wasn't to scare us but to get in position to do something worse. This building is basically a free-for-all. And Marianne said this floor was empty."

Cash drew his weapon and scanned the open area. To their left was a door that led to a stairwell and to the right was a long hallway. He rubbed his chin. "We could go straight to the stairs but if we are being played into a trap, the killer might be waiting in the stairwell. But we're law enforcement and might suspect that so the killer may be on either end of the hall. Or it's a psychological move and he's not here at all."

"This feels like which cup to drink from in *The Princess Bride*." Mae's heart beat against her ribs. "Both were poisoned."

"Great," Cash deadpanned and slipped toward the door leading to the stairwell.

SEVEN

Cash wiped sweat from his brow with the back of his hand and peered through the small square window into the stairwell. One set of concrete stairs went up and one went down. Both looked clear but that didn't mean they couldn't be ambushed on either set.

They had three choices to exit. The killer couldn't be in all places at one time. He glanced at Mae and she was peeping into the hall.

"Looks clear on both sides, but who knows what lies behind any of those office doors or the other stairwells," she whispered.

The question was, had someone set this whole thing up? Who would have known they were coming here if they weren't followed—and Cash couldn't say with certainty that they hadn't been tailed. Anyone at the station knew they were coming over. The killer chose to stall out the elevator, knowing how to switch breakers or control panels. Also someone had to know that the second floor was empty. Could be anyone. It was no secret to anyone in Willow Banks that Jenner Elevator was closing.

"Cash?" Mae hissed. "Give me something here."

"There's too many offices to clear. While the stairs are tight, we have a better chance at firing back and if we have blind spots, the killer does too."

Mae agreed.

"Cover me." Cash pushed open the door, keeping his back flush to the wall as he aimed his gun upward until he came to the stairs leading to ground level, then he switched aim below him as Mae kept her gun trained on the stairs above them. He caught her eye and motioned with his chin toward the next set of concrete stairs and nodded that he was going to head down them. She returned the nod.

The stairwell had great acoustics, so as quiet as they were trying to be, the sound of shoes scuffing along concrete echoed. Cash's pulse pounded.

He kept to the wall and not the railing, inching down one step at a time.

Mae was a few feet behind him, covering his back.

One step.

Two steps.

His heart rate slowed as the door to the first floor came into view. If the killer was messing with their minds, he was doing a bang-up job.

Cash peeped through the glass. The lobby area appeared clear. "I think we're—"

Gunfire exploded and sparks on the metal railing burst into the air. Cash's ears rang. Mae ducked and fired back. The shots had come from the stairs above. The killer must have been on the third-floor stairs, heard them moving and crept down.

Another shot fired. Mae winced and fired another round. Oh no. "Mae, are you hit?" She was in the crosshairs and hurt. Red seeped through her pale blue dress

Loyal Readers
FREE BOOKS Voucher

We're giving away **THOUSANDS** of **FREE BOOKS**

Romance

Suspense

Get up to 4
FREE FABULOUS BOOKS
You Love!

To thank you for being a loyal reader we'd like to send you up to 4 FREE BOOKS, absolutely free.

Just write "YES" on the Loyal Reader Voucher and we'll send you up to 4 Free Books and Free Mystery Gifts, altogether worth over $20, as a way of saying thank you for being a loyal reader.

Try **Love Inspired® Romance Larger-Print** books and fall in love with inspirational romances that take you on an uplifting journey of faith, forgiveness and hope.

Try **Love Inspired® Suspense Larger-Print** books where courage and optimism unite in stories of faith and love in the face of danger.

Or **TRY BOTH!**

We are so glad you love the books as much as we do and can't wait to send you great new books.

So don't miss out, return your Loyal Reader Voucher Today!

Pam Powers

LOYAL READER
FREE BOOKS VOUCHER

YES! I Love Reading, please send me up to 4 FREE BOOKS and Free Mystery Gifts from the series I select.

Just write in "YES" on the dotted line below then return this card today and we'll send your free books & gifts asap!

➡ ___ YES ___ ⬅

Which do you prefer?

☐ **Love Inspired®
Romance
Larger-Print**
122/322 IDL GRJD

☐ **Love Inspired®
Suspense
Larger-Print**
107/307 IDL GRJD

☐ **BOTH**
122/322 & 107/307
IDL GRJP

FIRST NAME | LAST NAME

ADDRESS

APT.# | CITY

STATE/PROV. | ZIP/POSTAL CODE

EMAIL ☐ Please check this box if you would like to receive newsletters and promotional emails from Harlequin Enterprises ULC and its affiliates. You can unsubscribe anytime.

LI/SLI-520-LR21

▲ If offer card is missing write to: Harlequin Reader Service, P.O. Box 1341, Buffalo, NY 14240-8531 or visit www.ReaderService.com ▲

FIRST-CLASS MAIL   PERMIT NO. 717   BUFFALO, NY

BUSINESS REPLY MAIL

POSTAGE WILL BE PAID BY ADDRESSEE

HARLEQUIN READER SERVICE
PO BOX 1341
BUFFALO NY 14240-8571

NO POSTAGE
NECESSARY
IF MAILED
IN THE
UNITED STATES

shirt. Cash threw open the door to the lobby and he and Mae burst through.

Going back in and giving chase was too dangerous. He wouldn't risk Mae's life and she'd already been hit.

"I'm fine." She breathed in sharply at the pain. Right now, there was nothing he could do for her. "There's no way out of the building except on the first floor and there are a dozen exits at least." They were only two people and couldn't cover them all.

"Split up." Mae wasn't a weakling. She was tough and capable and while it terrified him letting her go alone, he trusted her to do the job she'd been trained to do. Cash scrambled toward the front sliding doors.

"I'll check the back lot!"

Cash ran to his car and grabbed the radio on his dash. "Delta 3 SO."

"Delta 3 go ahead."

"Shots fired at 2120 Nail Road. Jenner Elevator. Suspect last seen leaving the stairwell in the northeast corner of the first floor of the main building. I need backup to the northeast corner and a perimeter set up. Advise Magnolia PD if they can assist. Send an ambulance. An officer has been hit but is stable. I repeat is stable."

Out front, only the cars he'd noted earlier were in the spaces. He blew around the side of the building, meeting Mae in the back lot. Empty.

Either the shooter got away on foot or was running to his vehicle now. Woods surrounded the south end and on the other side of the road was a small subdivision.

Three deputies from the SO along with the city PD barreled into the lot and one of his CID colleagues, Waylon Becker, drove in from the other direction a few moments later in his unmarked. What was he doing on this end of town? Cash was only glad he was.

He relayed what happened again and they fanned out to search and clear the building of employees. Mae refused treatment until the search was over.

Twenty minutes later, Mae met up with Cash in the lobby and Waylon exited the stairwell with a grim expression. "Nothing," he said.

Cash kicked the pavement. They'd lost this guy again. "The breaker that controls the elevator was switched. So we know it was done on purpose and not a power outage. Especially since other areas of the building didn't lose electricity."

Mae frowned and eyed Waylon but responded to Cash. "I think he used the elevator to position himself."

"How's your shoulder?"

"Minor abrasion." Paramedics had responded and inspected the graze, cleaned and patched it.

Deputy Anderson drove up and rolled down his window. "Nothing in the neighboring subdivisions. No one running. No one said they saw anyone."

The other deputy jogged up shaking his head. The small huddle of employees sat near the front entrance. Cash okayed them to go back inside but most of them declined and headed home.

Marianne waited until her coworkers were out of earshot. "Did this have anything to do with Harrison Trout?"

"I can't say for sure. I don't want to scare you but be extra cautious and keep your doors and windows locked." He retrieved his business card from his pocket. "Call me if you need anything, think of anything or get uneasy."

"Thank you, Detective Ryland." She grinned and gave him the eyes. The ones that said she was interested.

He dipped his chin and left the conversation at that then strode over to Mae. "How are you holding up?"

"Not as good as Marianne." She smirked. "I saw the look she gave you. That card you gave her business or personal?"

Cash's cheeks flamed. "Business. I—uh—don't have much time for romantic relationships these days."

"No?" She gave him a knowing look. He'd had a girl on his arm like strays to leftovers as a teenager.

"No." It wasn't worth getting close to someone only to have to end it. Not fair to the woman or to him.

Mae glanced at Marianne again. "She's pretty."

Cash shrugged. Didn't matter. "I'd like to talk to Harrison Trout. See what he's been up to this morning."

"See if maybe he's been shooting at us in stairwells?"

"Pretty much."

In about fifteen minutes, Cash had parked near the courthouse and they walked across the street to Harrison Trout's office, which was located in a two-story building. A railing on the top floor overlooked the street facing the courthouse. Harrison would have a great view of people—women in particular—coming in and out of the courthouse, shopping in boutiques or eating at the handful of restaurants on the square.

They entered and took the stairs to his office.

"If I never see a stair again…" Mae muttered as they climbed the wooden steps to Harrison's office. A young woman with tight curls and a welcoming smile greeted them. "How can I help you?" she asked.

"We'd like to speak with Mr. Trout, please," Mae said.

The woman nodded. "Sweet timing. He just arrived."

She noticed Cash's gun and badge on his belt. "I'll get him right away, Detective."

Cash and Mae exchanged glances. "Wonder where he's been?" Cash whispered.

Harrison Trout swaggered out in an expensive suit and an arrogant mug. "Detective Ryland, what brings you here? Troy's case?" Harrison eyed Mae; his pupils dilated. She was definitely Trout's type. Blonde. Blue-eyed. Pretty. Cash introduced her as Agent Vogel. Mae refrained from shaking his hand and kept it cool.

Trout's eyebrows rose and he motioned them into his fancy office. Sleek. Modern. "I'm guessing you don't need a defense attorney...or maybe you do."

"We're here about Tommy Leonard," Cash said.

"And Marianne Scott," Mae added.

Mae sat in the case room across from Cash. She rubbed her temples trying to thwart a headache. Their conversation had gotten them nowhere with Harrison Trout. He was an attorney and knew exactly how to word his statements and dance around questions he'd rather not answer. According to him, the restraining order had been due to a vindictive woman. He transferred to Mississippi for a fresh start. He had no answer for why two more women had filed complaints against him. He wasn't a mind reader.

He denied knowing Lisa Ryland but Mae's gut warned her he wasn't being honest.

Cash hung up the phone. "Troy is making progress. Tommy Leonard is still in solitary."

Harrison denied having a conversation with Tommy Leonard about Troy but the logs showed he called him the day of the attack. He was checking in—so he said. Mae wasn't buying it.

"Let's discuss the DNA under Lisa's nails. It belonged to Troy. If he was framed who would know how to get DNA—skin no less—from Troy and slip it under Lisa's nails without leaving any trace evidence of their own? And how did they accomplish it?"

"Particles from a skin scraping would be all that was required and if he were drugged he'd have never noticed. It wouldn't have left a mark. This is all stuff Harrison Trout should have brought up in court, but he didn't. And he'd know. Anyone in the justice system or fans of forensic shows and documentaries would. TV makes it easy for criminals. Easier anyway." Cash finished his cup of coffee.

They'd worked hard all day. Interviewed Kelly Wetzell, who told a story eerily similar to Marianne's and Tamera's. Except that Kelly had met Harrison while at the gym. Fitz Leeman, the divorce attorney next door, was unaware of Harrison's behavior but he'd had women feel uncomfortable after encountering him outside the offices. Fitz had been out of town the night of Lisa's murder and it could be corroborated so he was off the hook.

"Dinner wore off an hour ago," Cash said. "You want a doughnut or something? They're probably stale but…"

"No, I'm fine."

"I'm gonna go get one. Pretend it tastes good."

Mae stood and stretched her tight muscles, yawning as her cell phone rang. Lauren Jenkins. Oh no. Grandma Rose. She hurried and answered. "Lauren, is everything okay with Grandma Rose?"

"Oh yes, yes, sorry to alarm you. She's doing well.

Stable. She's alert and less disoriented." She paused a few seconds. "You mentioned if I needed anything or if something else happened to let you know…with the gifts." She cleared her throat. "Well, I just received an edible arrangement. My favorite—chocolate strawberries and salted caramel apples. I always leave salted caramel dip in my fridge and on weekends, when I'm feeling in the mood I'll make the strawberries."

Mae frowned. Where was Lauren going with this? "Okay."

"Thing is we didn't date long enough for him to know this about me."

Mae's stomach lurched. "You think Billy's been watching you or been in your home?"

"Yes," she croaked. "What can I do about that? I mean he's a cop. Cops stick together, right? Like some kind of code."

Some did. From what she'd noticed, Billy seemed likable by his colleagues. "Not all of us. Not me."

"What can you do? I mean, I don't want to start anything—"

"He started this, Lauren. You are not to blame. I'll handle it. If one more gift comes, I want a phone call ASAP."

"What are you going to do?"

Mae stepped into the hall and strode toward the break-room area where the vending and drink machines were located. Several deputies and detectives were helping themselves. Billy right in the thick of it. "Don't worry about it. It'll be all right."

She ended the call as her temperature rose. What gave this guy—one who was supposed to be living by a moral code, one that helped others—the right to intrude where he wasn't wanted, to go after what wasn't his?

Billy exited the break room with a coffee and a packaged honey bun. Mae stepped into his path. He had a foot and half on her but she didn't care. He didn't intimidate or scare her. He paused and sidestepped assuming it was an accident but she blocked him again and his brow furrowed.

"Agent Vogel, can I help you?"

"Yes, actually you can. Have you contacted Lauren Jenkins in the past month? Sent her gifts?"

"How do you know Lauren?"

"We're old friends and I'm protective of her."

Billy's eyebrows scrunched. "Okay. Well, good for you. Our relationship isn't any of your business." He went to move around her again but she entered his space and poked her finger in his chest.

"When she's receiving unwanted gifts, it is my business and the law calls that harassment. Stay away from her. Don't call her. Don't send her another gift and don't you dare go anywhere near her property or so help me, you'll regret it."

Billy gaped then a deep flush crept up his neck and his eyes narrowed. "I'm not sure who you think you are or what you know, but I suggest you keep your weak threats to yourself and your nose in the case you came to actually investigate."

"And you—"

"What's going on here?" Cash asked, glazed doughnut in hand.

"You need to keep your little out-of-town pup on her leash before she runs after a car and gets hit," Billy said, his tone filled with fury.

"First of all—" Cash tossed his doughnut in the trash a few feet away and wiped the sticky glaze on his jeans as he stepped toward Billy "—she's a woman and a respectable law enforcer so your pup remark needs to be apologized for. Second—" he took another step and Billy backed up "—that sounds an awful lot like a threat not only to a woman but an officer of the law. You want to rethink that statement?" He leaned into Billy, with at least three inches on him in height. Billy peered up into Cash's eyes that were cold as ice. "I asked if you wanted to rethink that and apologize."

Billy tossed Mae a glance. "Sorry."

He slunk around Cash, who wasn't budging to accommodate Billy. When he was around the corner, Mae wasn't sure if she was angry or appreciative. Angry was definitely at the top of the line but not because he'd intervened as if Mae couldn't fight her own battles. She was angry because she was attracted to Cash despite that he'd secretly stolen her heart in high school, been her first kiss—which he had no idea about—and then robbed her of her essay and being number one. And that attraction, mixed with who he appeared to be now, only heightened his appeal.

Mae didn't want to feel anything for Cash but maybe a fair measure of contempt and team camaraderie to solve a case. Instead she stood there like a complete moron, speechless and probably moon-eyed.

The puzzlement in his deep blue eyes helped her none nor did his sandy scruff across a bad-boy-model face. She wasn't sure if she should kick him or kiss him. She wanted to do both and straighten his hair that was in disarray and added to the attraction. But that'd only be an excuse to touch him.

"Mae? Did I— did I overstep my bounds?" His sincere husky whisper nearly sent her oozing into his arms. "If I did, I'm sorry. I know you can handle yourself, could have put him in his place with all those big words that come out of that brilliant brain. But I just…I just couldn't have him talk to ya like that."

Why was he being so kind and compassionate?

The reason was there at the tip of her soul.

Jesus. She hadn't wanted to believe Cash had changed but there was simply no denying it anymore. He was chivalrous and sweet. Protective and yielding. Confident and shy all at once.

She blew a sigh and spun on her heel, turning the corner like it was on rails, and rushed into the ladies' room where she splashed cold water on her face and stared at her reflection in the mirror.

"Have you lost all your marbles, Mae Ellen Vogel?"

The commode flushed and Lilith stepped out grinning. "Maybe," she said with a twinkle in her eye.

Mae ran her hand in front of the motion-sensored paper towel holder and tore one off, dabbing her face. "I didn't realize anyone was in here."

"I'm getting overtime, which is usually not allowed but Angie Fickle is on maternity leave and I could use the money. I'm helping Vickie open a new home for abused women. Actually, it belonged to my great aunt. Big ole house over past Kirby Hill. It'll be safe and out of the way. Needs some fixing up."

"Awesome. Count me in for a donation."

"Thanks." She grinned. "So, what's got you losing your marbles? I heard about what happened at Jenner today."

"It was the worst and there I was stuck in an elevator

of all places. Anyway, that's not it." She glanced at the stall and didn't notice any feet underneath. "It's Cash."

"He driving you crazy?"

"Yeah, in a way I wish he wasn't. I know what he did to me in high school but it's pretty clear he's changed and—"

"And you're feeling all the feels." Lilith snickered and turned on the faucet. "I get it. Cash has always been a looker. I think he's decent but the fact that he's trying to get his brother out of prison is a bit unsettling." She pumped the pink soap and scrubbed her hands.

"The more we look into it, the more I think Troy might be innocent. At least of murder. He absolutely should have received his licks for abuse—and maybe this stint in prison has dried him out and taught him something. But he can't go down for a murder he didn't commit so someone else can get off squeaky clean. Doesn't Lisa deserve justice?"

Lilith waved her hand and the paper towel released with a grinding noise. "Of course. I wouldn't be in this line of work if I didn't think so. Do you have any new suspects? Wayne?"

"We're looking hard at Harrison Trout." Mae told her about his indiscretions.

"Gross." She turned her nose up and tossed the paper towel. "Look, I'm all for happily-ever-after. I hope you find it. Just…be careful. That's all I'm saying. Rarely do they come around."

Mae left the bathroom and met Cash at the desk. "I'm gonna call it a night."

He stood. "Okay. Be careful. We're being watched."

He didn't ask to follow her home or stake out her place. She admired that. "And to answer your question, no. You didn't overstep your bounds, Cash." Mae hurried to the parking lot and drove back to Grandma Rose's house. She walked in to the smell of lilac and baby powder which brought back many wonderful memories of her grandmother.

She locked the door behind her and laid her gun on the entryway table. Then she slipped off her shoes and padded to the kitchen. Grandma never was at a loss for food. She found an unopened package of ham steaks and grabbed a carton of eggs and a slice of cheese to whip up an omelet. After eating and getting ready for bed, she crawled into sheets with soft pink rose petals and drifted away until she jolted awake.

She wasn't alone.

EIGHT

Mae had the upper hand. Whoever was in her bedroom didn't know she was awake yet. Her heart hammered against her ribs.

Adrenaline pumped. She pretended to mumble in her sleep and shift, removing covers from hindering her surprise attack. Cracking an eye open, she saw the figure in black slowly approach. She swallowed and prayed for strength then sprang from the bed, hollering and charging the intruder.

She knocked the solid figure into the rocking ottoman. The attacker tripped and toppled backward. Mae didn't have time to cross back to the nightstand and grab her gun or phone. Instead, she darted toward the kitchen and the closest door to exit the house. The intruder was hot on her trail. She grabbed a lamp and tossed it behind her, not sure if she hit her mark, but a low grunt said she did.

As she entered the kitchen the intruder grabbed the back of her hair and yanked her toward him. It felt like fire burning through her scalp and she shrieked as she fell onto the floor. Gloved hands wrapped around her throat and squeezed. It was dark and she could barely see the intruder's eyes from the ski mask. Were they light? Dark?

Mae grabbed at the hands, then reached up and went for the eyes. The attacker must have anticipated her self-defense move and reared back, releasing some pressure from Mae's throat. She bucked and threw him off balance then grabbed the leg of the kitchen chair and swung it as hard as she could into the attacker. That released her completely from his grip and she scrambled to her feet and aimed toward the back door. She unlocked it with fumbling fingers and hustled into the backyard.

She zipped around the side of the house and noticed the garden hose rolled up on the stand. She yanked it and pulled it with her along the yard. Her pursuer was right behind her.

Mae tugged on the hose and heard a groan as the attacker tripped over it and crashed to the ground. Too far to double back and subdue the attacker—he'd be to his feet before she could make it and his solid mass outweighed her. Her best choice was to sprint across the street to Mr. Tuckett's home and call for help.

As she stormed out of the driveway into the street, headlights popped on and a car door opened. "Mae!"

Cash? "Cash!"

She ran straight for him. "Behind me! He's behind me! I don't have my gun."

Cash drew his SIG Sauer and ran toward the side of the house, only a fraction of a limp in his gait. Mae had no weapon so she waited while frantically pacing beside the mailbox.

What was Cash doing here?

She braced as a figure rounded the house. Only Cash.

He jogged to the car. "He's in the wind. I made a pass through the neighbors' yards. What happened?"

She told him.

He smirked. "Smart thinking making a play for him before he attacked you in the bed." His glance moved down her torso and legs and back up, meeting her eyes. She was in a long T-shirt and a pair of short shorts she liked to sleep in.

Instead of feeling creeped on, her insides flushed hot and her mouth turned achingly dry. "I, uh—should get back inside."

His right eyebrow lifted and the way he held her gaze. Now she understood the "weak in the knees" concept she'd read about in romance novels. Not that she read a lot of them.

"What are you doing here, Cash?"

He leaned into the car and plucked out her purse. "Thought I'd bring this by?" It was a question. As in was she buying the story? No. But man, she couldn't be mad that he'd been staking out her place.

The awareness of how near he was, how masculine, whopped her upside the heart and sent it skidding into her head and taking it for a swirling spin. She reached out and clasped the purse. "I guess I owe you a thanks." Her voice was soft and hoarse, full of emotion and anticipation. Of what? She wasn't sure.

He didn't release the handle and her fingers brushed his, sending wild excitement through her middle. "I guess so," he murmured all low and husky. "For the purse or running off your intruder?"

She couldn't help but grin when a killer in their midst was no laughing matter but the air crackled between them and the heady feeling pushed out all notion to be afraid or wary.

She let her index finger brush across his knuckles and his eyes slightly widened and the smirk turned alluring. "I guess both."

"Well, Mae," he drawled, slow and thick like honey dripping from the comb on a hot June day, "you're most welcome."

He held her gaze, confidence and the big question right there whirling in his dark blues. She ran her top teeth across her bottom lip—her answer.

Cash released the purse and cupped her cheek, searching her eyes as he closed the distance between them. His minty breath enveloped her senses and his lips grazed hers. The feather-soft touch was barely there and her pulse spiked.

"Who's out there?" a sharp voice hollered and a porch light glared in Mae's eyes.

Mae darted away and cupped a hand over her eyes, straining to see Mr. Tuckett across the street. "It's me, Mae, and Detective Ryland."

"Oh, I didn't know what was going on. The headlights are shining in my bedroom. Woke me up."

"I'm sorry, sir." Cash reached inside the car and cut the lights.

Mr. Tuckett grunted his reply and went inside, leaving them alone and the moment gone.

"I should go," Cash said. "Hey, would you want to go to Judge Pendergrass's cocktail party and fundraiser with me Friday night? It'll give us a chance to snoop."

Mae smiled. "For a second I thought you were asking me on a date."

Cash cocked his head. "If I did would you have said yes?"

She hoisted her purse onto her shoulder. "I guess we'll never know," she flirted. "Thanks for bringing me my purse."

"I wanted to make sure you were safe."

"I know. See you in the morning."

"Let me help you clear it before I go."

She nodded and they did an outside sweep then inside. All clear. She locked the back door and walked Cash to the porch. "Go home for real, Cash. Get some sleep. We're on alert and he knows it. It'll be okay." She hoped but that cold dread roiled in her stomach.

He pointed to the door. "Lock that up, please." He winked and went down her porch steps backward, keeping his eyes on her. Once he made it to the sidewalk, he turned and jogged to his unmarked.

Mae closed and locked the door then peeped from the curtains as the car engine started. Cash Ryland was going to kiss her. For a second time. And she was going to let him. What did that mean?

He inched down the road with the lights off so not to disturb Mr. Tuckett. Thoughtful. She sighed and padded to the bedroom.

Was the cocktail party a date or not?

She lay in bed wide awake wondering about Cash's invitation and listening to every single pop and crack in the house. Could it have been Harrison Trout? Someone else? What about Billy Anderson? He might not have anything to do with Troy's case but he sure was fired up about her confrontation earlier this evening. Could he have been angry enough to come after her tonight—the car hitting the dog analogy? Guess he hadn't counted on a dog catcher lying in wait on the side of the street. But wouldn't Billy—being a deputy with the SO—have recognized Cash's unmarked outside her house? Maybe so. He had gotten in unbeknownst to Cash. If Mae hadn't escaped, she might be dead and Cash would still be out there clueless.

She didn't want to think about it anymore. She closed her eyes and forced herself to think of anything other than the attempts on her life. Before she drifted off to sleep a final thought hit.

What would she wear Friday night?

Cash pulled his Chevy Avalanche into Mae's Grandma's narrow driveway and adjusted the black bow tie on his tux. He was a flannel-and-work-boots kind of guy not penguin-suits-and-shiny-shoes guy, but it was only once a year and for an important cause.

The sky was gray and swollen. The temperature had dropped in just an hour as a storm from the Gulf Coast pushed a cool front through and with it—thunderstorms. They might get rained out of the event—though Pendergrass's home could fit them all inside if necessary.

Wind jostled his truck.

Maybe he should have borrowed his mentor's Acura. Mae would be all gussied up and climbing in his big truck in heels wouldn't exactly be graceful. His nerves hummed and vibrated through his body. Was this a date? She'd been vague but her eyes held flirtation and allure.

But the day after their almost-kiss, she'd been awkward and cautious. He got that. She'd been wary when he'd asked for tutoring back then too, and as the weeks went by, she'd relaxed around him and they'd talked about more personal things and shared a few laughs and burgers. A week before he'd stolen her essay, they'd walked home from the library and under the big magnolia tree at the corner of her street, he'd gathered the courage and taken her hand.

Mae, thanks for helping a dumb guy like me, he'd said.

You're not dumb, Cash. You're not at all what I expected—not that I expected dumb. She'd blushed and nervously laughed.

I'm not? What did you expect? Something about her had made him want to be a cleaner version of who he was. He'd worked to keep from cursing and he hadn't smoked before seeing her or when he was around her. Nasty habit anyway.

I don't know. She kicked her toe along the spring grass and ran her top teeth across her bottom lip. It undid him. But it wasn't her beauty that drew him—well, it was at first but the continued draw came from her kindness and generosity. She was helpful and patient. Witty and also feisty. *A player, I guess.*

He'd been a player for sure. But not with her. *I get that. But, Mae...* He'd lifted her chin to peer into her eyes. He'd wanted her to know—to see in his eyes—how truthful he'd been in that moment. *I've never played you. Besides, you'd be too smart to fall for it.* Her high cheekbones had been sharp, her skin velvety as he'd caressed it with his thumb. *You're not what I expected either.*

A big nerd? Or what Landon Murry told the whole school I was when he stole my underwear. Tears had glossed over her eyes and the blush deepened.

Landon Murry had been nothing but a two-bit jock

with money. Cash had never believed him and when he'd heard Mae had punched him, he'd been proud and intrigued. *No, just smart and pretty and kind. I—I've never met a girl like you, Mae. I'm not sure I ever will*, he'd murmured as he leaned his arm above her head and rested it on the tree branch.

Are you gonna kiss me?

Would that—would that be okay?

She'd swallowed hard and barely nodded. The sweetness and innocence moved him. She was everything he wasn't. Everything he wished to be. She deserved to be kissed thoroughly but tenderly. For the first time in his life, he'd been nervous about kissing a girl.

Because Mae hadn't been just any girl.

He couldn't screw this up. He'd carefully made his way to her lips, giving her the chance to change her mind. Kissing her was a highlight for him, but he wasn't anybody she ought to be kissing.

She'd been unsure at first and so had he. It was like he'd never kissed anyone before. But as he'd cradled her delicate face, he'd found his footing and led her through the purest, most honest kiss he'd ever experienced.

When he broke away before it led to something more passionate—something that would taint the goodness in it, she stood with her eyes closed and a close-lipped grin.

He'd chuckled and tweaked her nose, then slid her hair behind her ear. They silently walked to her home, their hands touching but not locked. That's how it had been the past couple of days as they worked together. Not discussing what had almost happened but not quite as distant anymore. He wasn't sure where they stood. He knew where it ought to be—nowhere.

A crack of thunder snapped him from his thoughts. Should he walk to her front door? Text her he was here? His brain and heart were muddied. Getting involved with Mae would only kill him in the end. And maybe her too.

He'd hurt her enough.

The light in her eyes had dimmed in his presence after he'd betrayed her. But last night, he caught the first hints of that same former brightness glowing in her eyes.

He scratched the back of his neck then hauled an umbrella from the back seat and marched to the front door. As he lifted his fist to knock, she opened it.

Only a piece of glass separating them—a thin but needed barrier to keep from sweeping her into his arms and replaying that kiss under the magnolia tree. She was in a strapless, flowy black dress with a pendant made of little fake diamonds at her waist. It touched just above her knees with a little flair. Her hair was parted in the middle and fell to her collarbone in soft curls he ached to get lost in. She wore darker makeup but her lips only shimmered their natural color.

His throat ached and he swallowed. "Wow. You look amazing, Mae." It could pour down buckets right now and he wouldn't even care.

She grinned and a soft blush colored her cheeks. "Thank you." She opened the glass door and let her gaze sweep over him. "You belong in Hollywood, not Willow Banks, Cash." Her eyes focused on his truck. "No unmarked tonight?"

"No."

Maybe because he had wanted it to be more of a date than investigation. "That okay? I should have brought the car. The truck's kind of high." He escorted her to passenger side, the wind whipping her hair. He awkwardly placed his hands on her trim waist to help her onto the rail and inside. Her cheeks turned a deeper shade of red and she cleared her throat.

"Thanks. I like the truck. Smells great in here."

"I didn't spray anything."

She caught his eye and her finely arched eyebrow slowly raised. "Smells like you."

Oh boy. This night was going to be difficult to get through without wanting more than a working partnership. He couldn't—wouldn't hurt Mae ever again. He held her gaze until he hit the edge of sanity telling him not to jump in and kiss her mindless. One more second and he'd ignore that warning. He tossed her a flirty grin and closed the door.

God, don't let me mess this up. Don't let me hurt her.

He drove off the main highway into the hills that led out of town where Judge Vickie Pendergrass's estate was located. A fresh blacktop drive wound through the hills to her spacious home with floor-to-ceiling windows covering the front and the back. Even from here, the glow of small lights hung and swayed in the trees as the wind gusted.

They pulled into her circle drive, winding around a nine-tier fountain that bubbled and glowed in a rock garden. A valet took the keys from Cash and he rounded the back of the truck and stood next to Mae.

"Wow. Swanky," Mae said. "We're probably gonna get wet, though."

A string quartet's music filtered through the sticky night air. Servers dressed in black and white held trays of champagne as they entered the foyer. High ceilings, highfalutin and high society all congregated to converse and probably compare each other's success.

Mae and Cash passed on flutes of bubbly and surveyed the scene. Wayne Furlow stood in his fancy penguin suit—a fat silver tie hanging rather than a bow tie—with a glass of wine from the open bar and a brilliant smile on his face as he chatted with a blonde.

"Let's make a pass outside, see if other persons of interest are here and then we can head upstairs where the silent auction items are. Maybe bid on a tropical vacation. I sure could use one," Cash muttered.

"Amen. Me too."

"You hear any news today from the hospital?"

Mae had been working the case and visiting her grandma on lunch and dinner breaks. He wished there was something he could do. The concern and heartbreak in her eyes as she had to watch the woman's decline ate him up like tonight's stormy clouds were eating the sky.

"She might get to come home in a few days but she'll be wheelchair bound. My dad and Barrett have been discussing assisted living. But she'll hate that. Her mind is sharp and she's actually getting mobility back."

They walked out the French doors. A huge figure-eight pool with a hot tub and waterfall surrounded by rich stone set center stage. Floating lanterns drifted lazily in the tropical-blue-lagoon water. The quartet played under a lit gazebo and a crowd of people danced under a huge white tent, enjoyed appetizers and conversed at tables with white cloths and white wooden chairs.

"She spares no expense."

Cash clucked his tongue against his cheek. "I see Harrison Trout." He pointed across the lawn to a quieter area near a row of pale pink crepe myrtles. Trout had the ear of a county clerk and his finger brushed across her wrist in an intimate gesture. The woman's smile was tight and she shifted to remove contact. "You seein' what I'm seein'?"

"Yep. This guy is on the top of my list. He's a creep regardless."

"Agreed."

"Do you think we look too cop-like?" she asked.

His gaze swept over hers and the breath left his lungs. "The last thing you look like tonight is a law enforcer, but we could blend better." Cash motioned with his chin to the music. "You want to dance?"

"And scan as we turn circles?"

Brushing a strand of windblown hair from her cheek, he leaned in. "Or...we could just dance," he whispered. This was not keeping distance. Not holding back.

"We could do that," she said and accepted his open hand. He led her to the quieter edge of the black-and-white-checkered dance floor. With his left hand, he lightly embraced her lower back—soft and strong—pulling her against him, then he laced his right hand with hers, drawing their intertwined fingers to his chest. When her free hand lay flush on his upper back, his stomach jumped. Dainty but perfect fit.

She peered into his eyes. "I can't tell you the last time I danced... Actually it was at my unit chief's wedding and it was the Chicken Dance."

"Da-ta-da-ta-dah-to-dah," he sang through a breathy chuckle, imagining her clucking and twisting to the song. "No one asked you to slow dance?"

"Nope."

"I find it hard to believe a man who wasn't dead or

painfully shy wouldn't leap at the opportunity to have you in his arms—if only for a few minutes of a song." Which was about the amount of time he had with her and he planned to sop it up, though it was selfish.

He enjoyed the pink blush in her cheeks and she dropped her gaze, then in sober truth cast her eyes back on him. "I'm not good— I'm not— I have trouble with relationships." The shade of embarrassment replaced her blush and that shade wasn't enjoyable, but disheartening. "It's hard for me to trust men."

Cash had known that early on, but he had no idea it ran deep enough to bar her from a romantic relationship. "I'm sorry." He'd been a contributor to her guardedness. "I'm sure it'll come along for you at some point." But not with him and that sent a ripping streak of green through him. He wasn't sure she'd ever trust him personally and even if she did…he couldn't act on it. Not when a woman like Mae probably would want children and with his dyslexia, he had a high chance of passing that on to his children.

"I don't think so. What about you? Why aren't you settled down? You still playing the field?"

"I wouldn't even know where the field is these days."

She studied him, pierced him with her stunning eyes. "I'm sure it'll come along for you at some point."

He grinned at his words she tossed back to him.

Lightning flashed and shrieks sounded. But it illuminated two people near the trees.

"Hey, look," Cash said.

Judge Joe Sharp had a tight grip on Judge Pendergrass's forearm. She tugged free and thrust her finger in his furious face.

Judge Sharp towered over her, his mouth moving

at a fast pace. Thunder pealed and lightning streaked along the black sky. Drops of chilly rain dotted Cash's forehead and Judge Pendergrass stalked toward the side door.

"Let's get in before we get drenched and check it out." It may have nothing to do with Troy but the judge had put hands on her and not in a consenting or pleasant way. Now he was chasing after her. Cash's gut rolled over.

Something sinister was coming with the storm and a chill broke out on his arms.

NINE

Mae sprinted with Cash across the thick, perfectly manicured lawn in her heels. The drops became pelts as thunder rocked the night and lightning lit it up like noonday sun.

Chancellor Pendergrass had rushed in the side door of her house with Chancellor Sharp in hot pursuit. What could they possibly be fighting about? The side door opened to an empty study, full of polished wood, glass and law books.

"Where'd they go?" Cash inspected the room.

"I don't know." She poked her head into the hall. One end led to the formal dining room where guests had gathered to stay dry. The other hall led to a staircase. "Let's go upstairs."

They climbed the wooden stairs that slightly spiraled to a loft. Muffled voices came from a guest room. Not too many people had found their way upstairs. Most were milling downstairs or taking shelter under the large white tent outside.

"That's Chancellor Pendergrass's voice," Mae whispered as they eavesdropped.

"Are you sure you're okay, Sheila? How many times

are you going to let Joe do this to you?" Chancellor Pendergrass asked.

"He's under a lot of pressure, Vick. Lilith, you know. You've worked in his courtroom." Chancellor Pendergrass was talking to a woman named Sheila, who must be Chancellor Sharp's wife. Lilith was also in the room and acquainted with Sheila. If the way Sharp grabbed Pendergrass outside was any indication of how he treated his wife, then the chancellor and Lilith were discussing domestic abuse from an upstanding judge in the chancery court.

"Sheila, that's not an excuse." Lilith's voice reached Mae's ears. Soft. Concerned. "No pressure on earth should ever result in bruises and a broken wrist, which you've had on more than one occasion. We all know they weren't tennis accidents."

Mae and Cash exchanged glances.

"What are you two doing?" A sharp, deep voice cut through their moment and Mae turned to see the respectable Chancellor Sharp standing in his tuxedo, mouth taut and fire in his eyes.

"What have you been doing? That might be the better question," Mae said.

Chancellor Sharp glowered, not a single hair out of place. Lilith stepped from the room. "Chancellor Sharp."

He gave her an equally evil eye. "Where is my wife?"

He knew exactly where she was.

"Why don't you cool off and we can talk," Lilith said and stepped forward. She was serious. Mae wouldn't want to tumble with her, and with her passion for helping abused women, Chancellor Sharp better think twice.

"You don't tell me what to do."

"I will," Chancellor Pendergrass commanded, strong and able in her own right, as she stepped into the hall and closed the door behind her. "This is my house. Be thankful Sheila is one of my dearest friends or I'd have you thrown in jail already. Not here pretending to be an honorable judge."

Chancellor Sharp glanced at Mae and Cash then back to Chancellor Pendergrass. "You have no idea what you're talking about. This vindictiveness has to stop. I'm the senior judge and that won't change."

Chancellor Pendergrass's eyes darkened like the storm outside. She went from sophisticated and classy to murderous. Mae shuddered and laid her hand on her thigh holster where she'd tucked her gun. "This has nothing to do with your seniority or—" She straightened when she realized witnesses—law official witnesses, at that—were listening and she regained her composure. "You'll need to leave the second floor or I'll have Deputy Freedman escort you out."

Lilith didn't seem to mind that duty.

Cash cleared his throat. "Sir, maybe a few minutes to cool off isn't such a bad idea."

Thunder cracked and rattled the windows. The power flickered.

Chancellor Sharp glared hard at the closed door behind which his wife was hidden away—from him. "This is far from over. Mark my words."

"You don't want to threaten me, Joe," Chancellor Pendergrass said through a quiet but venomous tone.

He spun on his heel and stomped down the hall toward the theater room where a few other men had gone when the moment had heated. The few that had continued to linger nearby didn't seem to notice Chancellor Pendergrass and Chancellor Sharp in their tense positions.

"What is going on?" Cash asked.

Chancellor Pendergrass breathed a sigh and her shoulders relaxed. "Nothing that concerns you, Detective." She marched back inside the room.

"Lilith?" Mae asked.

"I imagine whatever you're thinking is true."

"Did Lisa know about Chancellor Sharp's ugly secret side?" If she had, then maybe she approached him.

Lilith pinched the bridge of her nose. "This goes further than you think, Mae. Vickie started her program *because* of Sheila. She wanted a safe place for her oldest and dearest friend to take refuge in. But Sheila refuses to leave Joe. He does so much good. Blah, blah, blah. He can't ever run for supreme court justice if his family doesn't stick together. One pathetic excuse after another."

"Does anyone else know about his dark side?" Mae asked.

"Probably anyone who works closely with him, but no one breathes a word." Her upper lip snarled. "Go look at Chancellor Sharp's divorce cases. He's for the man. But Lisa got everything. You have to wonder why."

Cash and Mae once again exchanged glances. Cash rubbed his chin. "If Lisa knew about Judge Sharp's behavior, she could have used it as leverage to get everything including the boat. Troy was in an uproar because he thought he was losing everything—"

"He deserved to," Lilith stated sharply.

Cash blew a heavy breath. "I understand. I do."

Lisa might have gone a step further than leveraging

a divorce or maybe the chancellor anticipated increased blackmail. That alone would be motive for murder.

The wind howled against the windows and the lights flickered again.

"I need to get back to Sheila and Vickie." Lilith left them in the dimly lit loft area.

"Lisa had been on an expensive vacation and to a spa in Memphis before she died. Where did she get the money for that?" Cash's thoughts mimicked Mae's.

"Extortion?"

"Maybe. Troy felt he'd been slighted because Judge Sharp knew Lisa. Putting him in prison would shut him up and killing Lisa…"

"Definitely shut her up. Can we prove it was him?"

"We can run the trail and try. I saw a few guys I know who are divorced and Sharp was the judge. Good place to start."

"I'll take a run at Sheila. If he's hiding one thing, he may be hiding other things she knows about."

Rain pelted on the roof and thunder shook the house again. So much for a lovely night outdoors. Cash took off down the stairs and Mae knocked on the bedroom door. "It's Mae. Can I come in?"

The lights flashed again and when they flickered back on, she spotted the redhead that Harrison Trout had gotten a little too friendly with outside. She might be worth talking to. Mae hadn't ruled him out.

Chancellor Pendergrass opened the door. "Agent Vogel, there's nothing for you to do in here. I'll take care of Sheila and I can take care of Joe too." The steely tone put Mae on edge. What exactly did that mean?

The chancellor shut the door in her face before she could utter a response and the power completely went out and threw them into darkness. Groans and curses resounded from the theater room and downstairs. She turned on her cell phone flashlight. The redhead had vanished and the loft had been cleared.

Suddenly it felt eerie and hollow.

Holding up the light, she hunted for the redhead. She couldn't have gotten far. The loft narrowed into a hallway with several rooms on either side. "Hello!" she called.

She poked her head inside and used the dim light to search for the woman. Where could she be?

Mae's phone light cast creepy shadows along the walls as she inched toward the stairs. Might as well find Cash. She had gotten nowhere fast.

Hairs rose on her neck.

Before she could turn, a solid hand gripped her shoulder and shoved her forward.

Mae shrieked, unable to regain her balance. Her phone fell with a clatter and she tumbled after it, flailing and twisting to grab the rail and break her fall, but it was dark and she only clutched air.

As she pitched forward she knocked her shoulder into the wrought iron railing. She crashed onto her side as she hit the wooden stairs, momentum jostling her down each one with aching force until she smacked into the wall on the rounded landing, nailing her head against the hardwood.

Everything ached and wetness layered her cheek. She touched it and blood smeared her fingers. An explosion in her head sent her straight into darkness.

Cash frowned into the pitch black and kept on guard. All the suspects in Lisa's case were present, and darkness made a convenient canopy for crime. He'd been a target already.

So had Mae. His pulse spiked as he worked through the crowd of people continuing their evening in merriment—some complaining and muttering about needing a generator.

The house felt like something straight out of a murder-mystery movie. Lightning gave glimpses of shadowy light along with cell phone lights. Thunder foreshadowed doom and the wind rattled the windows in an angry gesture to get inside.

He'd only talked with his CID colleague, Shane Nicholson. He'd divorced last year and made out like a bandit and had been pleasantly surprised at Judge Sharp's ruling. Before Cash could get more details, the power had petered out.

He wove his way to the foyer where people had exited for areas with more light and away from the rows of windows. Mae should be upstairs in the room off the loft. As he rounded the first section of stairs, he paused at the heap blocking his climb. Shining his light on the source, his heart rocketed and he sprang into action.

Mae!

He knelt beside her, hands shaking. Blood had matted her hair against her cheek. Her body was limp and lifeless, but she had a pulse. Couldn't be sure if anything was broken, though. She was missing a heel. "Mae." He lightly touched her face. "Mae, can you hear me?"

A soft moan escaped her lips and he sighed in relief.

"Mae, it's Cash." They'd only been separated for about ten minutes. How long had she been lying here?

She raised up to sit and clutched the side of her head. "Ooh," she moaned again.

"Don't move. You might be hurt." He rested his hand on his shoulder. "Did you trip?"

"I wish. Someone shoved me. Someone strong."

Cash's concern skipped to fury. "Did you see who?"

"No," she said through a strained voice.

"I need to call an ambulance."

"Not a chance. I'm fine. I mean, I'm sore and bruised but I'll live. Check my head and see if it needs stitches. If not, I'm good to go."

"You passed out. You could have a concussion." She likely did. He used his light and delicately moved her hair—once blond, now dark with blood. She winced and he apologized.

"You have a cut but I don't believe it needs stitches. Head wounds bleed more. Are you dizzy?"

"No. I have a headache and I want to get cleaned up. If I feel dizzy or have blurred vision, I'll see a doctor. Promise. I'd like to stand now." He helped her to her feet.

"Woozy?"

"No. I need my shoe."

Cash shone his light and found it three steps up. He retrieved it and helped her balance while she slipped her dainty foot inside.

A downpour pummeled the roof and windows. "Let's find a bathroom."

"There's one upstairs and down the hall. I saw it when I was looking for the redhead Trout had been talking to. But she disappeared."

Cash carefully guided her up the stairs and into the bathroom. Inside, he rummaged through drawers and cabinets. No first-aid kit. Mae grabbed a washcloth and washed the blood from her face and neck.

"I can't see the cut," she griped into the darkness.

Cash rewet the rag and put his phone in her hand then lifted it and said, "Hold your hand here so I can see." He dabbed at her wound and worked to clean the blood from her hair but she'd need to wash it out more thoroughly at home.

Mae flinched and Cash paused. "I'm sorry," he whispered and thunder cracked. "Your hair looked real pretty tonight too."

A throaty laugh escaped her lips as she caught his gaze through the shadows in the mirror and held it. "Thank you." For the compliment or the help—or something else? There was a flicker in her eyes he couldn't read as he stood behind her, holding her hair from her neck with one hand and clutching a wet rag in the other.

He glided his knuckles down her cheek, letting them linger on her flawless skin as her eyes arrested him through the mirror. "You're welcome. I should have stayed with you."

"You had no idea."

"Still. I can't stand to see you hurt. And I keep thinking how I hurt you. I know I've apologized but it continues to nag me."

She touched his fingers that caressed her cheek and slowly pivoted to face him. The bathroom was small, and her nearness sent a thick wave of longing through him as awareness rippled in the air.

With light fingers, Mae grasped one of his lapels with her free hand then smoothed it as if it were rumpled. Her touch sent a fire through his gut clear to his throat, drying it out with an ache and turning his brain to sludge.

It was there in her eyes—that look. Longing mixed

with hope and anticipation. Fear and vulnerability. He dropped the rag in the sink, laced his fingers with hers and carefully—patiently—met her lips, a geyser of emotion exploding inside him.

At first, he simply sampled her mouth, allowing his rough lips to study the feel of hers—the Cupid's bow—the thicker lower lip. Silky. Smooth. A small gasp slipped past them, and her breath, tinged with a hint of cinnamon, consumed his mouth.

Cash cupped her cheeks in his hands, feeling the warmth pulse against his palms. He edged her against the sink, closing the distance between them, and shifted from sampling to savoring in deliberate detail.

She held nothing back in this kiss, laying it out bare and honest. He'd never experienced anything like this, never dreamed a kiss like this was possible. Never been moved and tortured all at once. It ran deeper than oceans and stronger than mountains but as gentle as a breeze and as soft as flower petals—the kind he'd picked for her once before a tutoring session. Tulips.

Mae Vogel—the fiercest, bravest, smartest woman he'd ever known. She was an inspiration and aspiration of all he desired to be. He pressed into the kiss, into everything she made him feel. In her arms, he was capable and confident. Secure and powerful. Her breath mingling with his fused him with life and energy. In this moment, Cash could scale a wall or hurdle the sea.

Unable to tear himself away, he was drawn into Mae's depths, a place he never wanted to leave.

Nothing but the sound of blended breath of two people who couldn't admit their feelings with voice but couldn't deny them in this display of affection. No doubt, he was affected. Down into the marrow of his bones. She'd glided her way there years ago and never left, only been silent.

He'd been awakened.

And he had no idea what to do with that.

They were well on their way to a full-blown make-out session when decency and common sense throttled him upside the brain and he broke away from the kiss.

She hadn't noticed he was bringing it to a necessary close.

"Mae," he whispered against her lips. "Mae," he breathed with more force, amused. He wasn't the only one affected, and his chest swelled with male ego—he wasn't immune to it—with the way he'd lit a fire in her. The fact that he knew he could—he found a healthy portion of self-centered satisfaction in that. "Mae," he repeated.

"What?" she murmured with her lips against his.

He glanced up and grinned. "We fogged up the mirror."

"What?" Confused and a little disoriented, which he also found pleasure in, she turned around and saw the mirror. "Oh."

"You want to draw a heart and put my initials in the middle of it?" he teased.

She smeared the glass with her hand and gave him a put-out look from her reflection. "No, and I don't want to doodle your last name next to mine on my interrogation notepads either."

"Ah, why not?" He playfully pinned her by holding the edge of the pedestal sink on either side. "Mae Ryland. You can even make the *A*'s little hearts." He chuckled then sobered. Mae Ryland sounded entirely too wonderful rolling off his tongue.

But she could never be Mae Ryland.

"Ha. Ha."

"Do you want kids?" he blurted. Maybe she didn't. And if that was the case then possibility soared. They could finish what they started at eighteen. What was forward movement just ten seconds ago.

"What? Not now," she said with a scrunched nose.

He chuckled. "I am an honorable man, thank you very much. I mean down the road. Do you want children?"

"One, you're scaring me and two, yeah. I'd like children if I ever married. But we talked about this…trust."

He'd felt complete trust in her kiss. One couldn't be that vulnerable and open without trust, could they? His heart sank regardless. "Oh. Okay. Well, now that I've sobered us both up so to speak, let's get out of here."

"You legit know how to throw cold water on a fire."

"Well, it was that or haul us into that shower, clothes on, and drench us in literal cold water." He laughed but nothing felt funny.

Mae wanted kids.

Cash wasn't ever having any.

Had he just made an even bigger, stickier mess than snatching an essay?

TEN

Saturday morning's weather wasn't cool, but it was less hot thanks to the storm bringing a slight reprieve. After leaving the bathroom and that kiss—one Cash couldn't shake—they'd left the party and he'd taken Mae home. He cleared her grandma's house, hated to leave but did without kissing her good-night.

Mae wanted children. That meant no more kissing. Even if she'd appeared disappointed. Stealing her heart was far worse than stealing a paper. He'd apologized for that but it felt weak. And it was after his first cup of coffee the idea struck him—a way to show deep remorse for the paper, for not being able to take that kiss to a more emotionally committed place.

It had sent him to the nearest Home Depot for supplies. He'd been at it for hours, never feeling lonelier than this moment as he hammered nails into the boards of the ramp he was building onto the front of Mae's grandma's house. He'd already built a wheelchair-accessible ramp in the back, which required tearing up some of the deck and rebuilding, but he didn't think Mae would mind. Or her grandmother. This might keep her from an assisted-living center for a while. If he needed to remodel the indoors, he'd do it, but not without prior permission. Overstepping bounds and all.

Cash had already overstepped last night even if the kiss had been consensual. He shoved the memory away and wiped the sweat from his brow. His stomach rumbled, reminding him he'd skipped lunch to finish the project before Mae arrived. It was nearly 7:00 p.m.

He'd only heard from her once—a text to mention Lauren had received another gift on her doorstep. Cash was going to have to make a stronger statement to Billy Anderson.

He threw a heap of extra lumber into the bed of his truck and began cleaning up the yard. Anyone could seamlessly wheel themselves up the sidewalk onto the ramp and to the front door where he'd extended the porch and awning so Rose and whoever might be pushing her wouldn't be cramped and could stay dry if it rained.

He was on his way to the truck with the last of his tools when Mae's black Jetta slowed in front of the house. Confusion knit her brow as she turned into the driveway. She exited the vehicle, gaping at the new construction. "Cash Ryland…" She threw her hands in the air. "I don't know what to say." She tested the ramp and ran her hands along the smooth wooden railing. "This is—amazing. You're a genius." The awe in her eyes swelled in his heart.

"I know Rose doesn't want to go to assisted living. This will help."

"What do I owe you? You have to let me pay you something," she said and admired it again.

The look on her face was payment enough.

"Mae, I owe *you*."

She held his gaze and tears welled in her eyes.

"There's a ramp in the back too. I had to reconstruct the deck, but I was hoping no one would mind."

She slowly shook her head then jogged around the side of the house and he followed.

"Oh my! I can't even!" She launched herself against him, wrapping him in a tight, thankful embrace. He probably smelled like a locker room, but he returned her hug anyway. She didn't seem to mind. And he enjoyed her sweet scent.

"I was happy to do it." To be a genius in her eyes. It was worth the aching pain and burn around his stitches.

She peered into his sweaty, dirty face. "There has to be something you want." Questions swirled in her eyes and her tone held skepticism.

"Mae," he said firmly, "I didn't do this for any other reason than that I wanted and needed to. No underlining motive."

"What? Underlying?"

"Yeah. The heat is boiling my brain." And he wasn't a genius at all. He was a fumbling goof who screwed up words on occasion.

She beamed. "Well, come inside for a cold drink. Better—let me make you dinner."

"I didn't do it for a meal."

"I believe you. But it's dinnertime. I'm hungry and you've got to be starving."

He was. But he was filthy. "Can I clean up first?"

"You don't have to on my account but if you want to…"

"I have a change of clothes in the truck. Can I use your bathroom?"

"Yeah. Come on."

He snagged his emergency bag. He never knew when he'd be delegated to a site when he was on call or on his off day. Inside, he cleaned up and rinsed his mouth with mouthwash then found her in the galley kitchen. It needed updating, but it oozed with hominess and Cash found it comforting.

The smell of tomatoes, onion and garlic hit his senses and his stomach responded.

"Spaghetti okay? It's quick and easy and I had ground beef thawed." The meat in the pan sizzled.

"It sounds perfect." He leaned against the sink and watched her use a wooden spatula to crumble the meat. "How's your grandma?"

"Better. They let me have more time than visiting hours. I had lunch with Mom and Barrett." She frowned. "He's convinced Troy is guilty. Can't explain the attempts on our lives but he encouraged me to go back to Batesville and work legit cold cases. He's so much like Dad. Know-it-all."

"How's your head?" he asked instead of responding about Barrett. He had no advice and she was only venting. Cash didn't mind being her sounding board.

"I've had a headache most of the day. I know I should be working but I admit I needed the day off." She lifted the pan from the burner and motioned for him to move aside so she could drain the grease. She dumped it in a colander and returned it to the skillet.

"I needed the day too. Sometimes working on something else helps clear my mind. I don't know how we can prove if Lisa blackmailed Judge Sharp—or even if she knew his secret. We can't prove if Wayne or Harrison was interested in her and became angry at unwanted advances. But Harrison has a pattern of stalking behavior with women. Wayne doesn't."

"But Wayne has more to lose if it turns out Troy is innocent."

"True but why kill us? All that will do is put the SO on his scent when investigating our murders." He watched her stir the boiling spaghetti. "Can I help with anything?"

"Nope." She grabbed two plates from the cabinet and set them on the old wooden kitchen table. When it was ready she brought the pot to the table then put the garlic bread on a plate and set it next to the pasta. "Bon appétit."

Sitting across the table from Mae and eating a meal felt more like home than it should. When his phone rang, he was relieved for the break, though the food was amazing and he was grateful for it.

"Detective Ryland."

He listened as Dispatch talked and his stomach sank. "No, I'm on my way now." He ended the call and turned to Mae.

"What is it?" she asked.

"I'm on call. I have to go and you'll want to come with me. Chancellor Joe Sharp is dead."

Mae left the plates, put the pot of spaghetti in the fridge and hopped into Cash's Avalanche. The chancellor's residence sat outside the city limits on a large estate. Only old-money houses out here. Police lights flashed ahead.

Cash gathered an evidence bag from his back seat. Mae grabbed her yellow legal pad. "Where's your notepad?" she asked. No way he could remember everything that was about to be said.

Cash held up a voice recorder. "I can't read my handwriting so I record it then get it on paper." His neck flushed red. He pressed the record button. "Call at 7:46 from Kiki Rogers in Dispatch to a homicide scene at 675 Helen Top Road. Chancellor Joe Sharp victim. Arrived on scene at—" he glanced at his watch "—8:01." He clicked the button and wiggled it in his hand.

She'd never seen a detective use a voice recorder. To each his own she guessed.

A first responding deputy met them at the front door. "I set up the perimeter with crime-scene tape. Joe Sharp was fifty-seven years old. Called the coroner and talked to the judge's wife, Sheila Sharp. She said they'd had a dispute and she hasn't been home since Friday afternoon. She came home this evening to get some clothes. Didn't expect him to be here. He usually has poker with a few friends on Saturday nights and I have their names written down. Found him in his study. Two bullets. One to the head. One to the chest."

Cash noted on his recorder that the scene was secure. Processing of the scene was already in play by the CSI team. Cash and Mae slipped paper booties over their shoes and gloves on their hands then made their way down the marble-floored hall to the scene.

"Nothing seems out of place," he said into the recorder.

Inside the study, Chancellor Sharp was slumped in his plush leather office chair. Cash took photos and described the scene into his recorder. He was proficient and sharp.

It smelled of pipe tobacco and death. French doors led out into a pool area and spacious backyard. Cash strode to the doors. Unlocked. "You do this or was it like this when you arrived?" he asked a CSI.

"Like that. I noted it and took photos."

He recorded it as a possible point of entry.

Mae studied the chancellor. He was still in his tuxedo from the cocktail party. That put time of death shortly after the event. He came into the study. A cigar that had burned down in the ashtray showed he'd lit one up recently. To work or think.

"No signs of a struggle." Mae frowned. "Either the shooter was invited through these doors or they were already unlocked by Chancellor Sharp. Did Mrs. Sharp come in through the front door or the garage entrance?"

The deputy who had been a first responder spoke. "She came through the garage. Said the alarm hadn't been set and that was odd. Sharp always set the alarm before bed."

Sharp came home from the cocktail party, probably irked about the events that occurred. Could even have been mulling over the fact that he shoved Mae downstairs—if it had been him; they might never know now. He came into his study before changing clothes or setting the alarm and was killed. In his chair. No struggle. "He knew his shooter."

Cash shared a knowing look with Mae. "He's well acquainted with his wife and she has motive."

Mae agreed. "Head and chest shot indicate an execution. Does Sheila Sharp know how to use a gun?" And would she be clever enough to attempt and mask the shooting as a professional hit?

"Let's find out."

Sheila Sharp hunched over a large marble breakfast bar in her pristine kitchen. The room smelled of lemon and pine-scented cleaner. "Mrs. Sharp," Cash said, "we're sorry for your loss." He held up his recorder and pressed Play. "Do you mind if I take my notes through audio?"

She shook her head.

"I need you to tell me verbally, ma'am."

"No, it's fine." Mascara clung to dark circles under her eyes. She held a ripped and crumpled tissue in her hand; her nose had been rubbed red and raw.

"Can you tell us what happened? I know you've already told it to the deputy, but we'll need to hear it too." He introduced Mae only as an MBI agent. Sheila didn't ask questions. She told them what the first responder had already conveyed.

"Is your husband a gun owner? Does he or you shoot much?" Cash asked. He was implying someone might have retrieved the weapon here, but Mae was aware what he was hunting for. Could Sheila use a gun and how well?

"He locks them up. Except for the one we keep upstairs. It's mine for protection when he's out of town. In my nightstand drawer."

Cash gave her a lopsided grin and she responded. Even a grieving woman couldn't resist that smile. "Having a gun by your bed only works if you can shoot it."

Sheila snorted. "Believe me. I can shoot. Joe made sure."

"Good to know."

She'd admitted she was a crack shot. Would a guilty person do that? Yes. That information would eventually leak. Better to admit it now than be caught in the lie later.

"Mrs. Sharp, I hate to ask this but where were you last night after the party?"

Sheila wiped her nose. "I expected this question. I am a judge's wife and he was a lawyer before he was a judge. I stayed at Vickie Pendergrass's. She can vouch for me."

"She see you all night long?"

Her eyes grew wary. "No. I slept in the guest room. I didn't kill Joe. I know you're aware of our situation and that gives me motive. But it wasn't me."

"Would you be willing to let me test your gun to see if it's been recently shot?"

"It has." She raised her chin as a challenge. "I was at the range Friday morning. You can verify that. T&J Gun Range in Memphis. I can get you the address if you need it."

"Not necessary, ma'am."

Convenient she had been at the range. If the gun she owned matched the bullets used to murder Chancellor Sharp, she wouldn't be looking pretty. They finished up and spent the next three hours assessing the scene, taking notes and collecting anything that might be evidence. Sheila's gun didn't match the weapon fired that killed Chancellor Sharp.

At half past midnight, they trudged to Cash's truck.

Mae yawned and leaned her head back against the seat. "I don't think the timing of his death was coincidence. Do you?"

Cash's scruff had thickened along his jawline and exhaustion filmed his eyes. "We can't say that it's connected to our case yet, but it's interesting that he died before we could question him about Lisa."

"So you don't think Sharp killed Lisa?"

"I don't know. If he killed Lisa, why kill him? He might have known something to help us aid Troy. It's like the real killer is taking out anyone who could advance our case." He adjusted the air. "Or maybe his death has nothing to do with our case. But I can't shake that it does." He pulled into her driveway. "How about we clear your house to make me feel better then we get some sleep. I don't know if you have a church home, but you're welcome to attend with me tomorrow— well, actually, this morning. Faith Christian. Starts at ten."

"I grew up at Christ's Fellowship." Mae had to admit she'd like to see Cash in a church setting. Not that she needed to see it to believe it. It was obvious. May be better if she *didn't* see him worshipping. Something was happening between them and seeing him sing to the Lord may defeat her in the tooth-and-nail battle she was fighting to keep herself safe.

The kiss at the party had breached her defenses. Her belly fluttered at the thought. The way he'd touched her with excruciating tenderness…he'd tasted like spearmint and security. The way his calloused fingertips had grazed her cheeks with reverence.

Then it was over and he was teasing her as if it hadn't been a potent experience. She didn't know what to think and if she asked it would mean she was interested in more and yet…that one moment of betrayal swung like an anvil reminding her he'd lied to her, used her, stolen from her and hurt her terribly. That hurt and mistrust idled quietly underneath many newly developed feelings and hope in his change, but if he'd done it once he'd do it again. Maybe not next week or next month or even next year but at some point, he could. She was too afraid to risk handing him her exposed heart.

But common sense lost this round. "I'll go with you. Thanks for offering." She climbed out of the truck with legs that felt like lead. Bone weary and ready for soft sheets, Mae unlocked the door. They cleared the house then she locked up behind him.

Chancellor Sharp was dead. She was going to church with Cash in a few hours.

Things surely couldn't get weirder.

ELEVEN

Sunday had only brought Mae more questions and confusion. She'd attended church with Cash and been welcomed by many—even met his mentor Charlie Child. She'd bumped into old classmates and all of that had been nice.

It was the sermon that had affected her in squirmy ways. A message on forgiveness. Forgiveness was flat-out hard when you didn't have the ability like God to throw the wrongdoing into a sea of forgetfulness. She hadn't forgotten what Cash did. She hadn't forgotten what Landon Murry had done or the way she was treated by his coach, the principal, teachers or even her father and brother.

It was like layer after layer of proof that trusting the opposite sex would end up a fatality of the heart. But that kiss and Cash's openness and honesty coupled with the way he'd protected her reputation and stood up to Deputy Anderson was of value and attested to his integrity. He'd been a teenager. She was aware of teenage mistakes. She'd made plenty of her own and wasn't holding it against herself. Cash was a grown man now.

She was a grown woman continuing to live in the

hurt of a teenage girl. That couldn't be healthy. But she didn't know how not to.

On this blazing-hot Monday morning, Mae glanced up from the computer she'd been using to sort through Lisa's social media and emails. She was searching for something that may connect Lisa to Chancellor Sharp and a link that proved Lisa knew his secret. But even so, that didn't prove Joe Sharp killed Lisa. Could be a step in the right direction at finding out who killed him and had been coming after her and Cash.

"Find anything?" Cash handed her a fresh cup of coffee. They'd been at the SO since nine this morning running leads, tracking people and finding nothing.

"No. We're missing a huge piece of the puzzle."

Cash collapsed in a rolling chair and righted himself. "Troy goes back to general population in a week. I'm afraid he won't last. We can't connect Tommy Leonard to Troy's stabbing but we can connect him to Harrison Trout. We know that Trout is a real piece of work and has stalked multiple women—possibly Lisa due to her reaction of him in the restaurant that day. He can be linked to Troy and to Lisa."

Mae liked Trout more than anyone for the murders, but they had no proof. "Wayne Furlow tried Troy's case, knew Lisa—flirted with her even—and would have a lot to lose if Troy was pardoned, but why would he have killed the chancellor?"

Cash sipped his coffee and cocked his head. "Joe might have known something that pointed to Wayne. And Wayne could have known about Joe's abusive behavior. Killing him could throw us off the investigation, caused more questions and eaten up the time I need to help Troy. This new homicide takes priority. All hands on deck."

All smart deductions. It would put the bulk of the case on her now. Not that Cash would stop investigating. He was tenacious. But if anyone knew how much time and manpower went into a homicide investigation it would be Wayne. "Okay, let's say he did kill the chancellor to sidetrack you and slow you down. He must have some serious confidence that the murder won't connect to him because it's a risky move."

"He could have hired someone anonymously on the dark web. That's pretty much impossible to track. He knows trace evidence. Whoever framed Troy did it up right."

True. "I'm a firm believer in Locard's exchange principle. When two objects meet, there is always a transference of one to the other. If Troy didn't kill Lisa, then where is the evidence of the person who did?"

"I can't be certain steps that should have been taken weren't. Something could have been missed."

"Soil samples? Did the killer float into Lisa's and then into Troy's without leaving any kind of particles from their shoes? We need to think like a killer," Mae said. "I'm certainly not a trained profiler and this case wouldn't warrant someone from the Behavioral Analysis Unit coming down from Quantico and offering their services, so it's up to us, Cash. Let's try to think outside the box."

His phone beeped and he read a text. "Be right back." He headed outside the workstations. Mae needed some sugar, and stale pastries from the vending station would have to do.

She rounded the corner and caught a glimpse of Teri,

Cash's deputy friend, beaming at him like he'd hung the moon. She'd become used to seeing those kinds of reactions he evoked.

"Teri, you're a gem if I haven't already told you that." His grin was ten thousand watts.

"Don't you forget it either." She handed him a stack of reports and he handed her his recorder. She pocketed it. "I'll have them all typed up for you in a few hours." She laid her hand on his forearm, her eyes almost hypnotized by his allure. "And you can do me a favor too," she purred.

"You name it."

"You know what I've been hoping for."

He chuckled low and throaty. "I think I can arrange that. Let's keep it on the down-low, though. We don't want rumors floating around."

"I think you know I can keep a secret, Cash Ryland. Your upstanding reputation is safe with me."

Mae's stomach dropped and her heart thundered in her chest. Once again, he was using his magnetism to get out of doing the hard work, the tedious work. Cash's winning smile and charisma had lowered Mae's guard in order for him to steal her essay. What was he trying to steal from Teri? Other than free work he didn't want to do. No wonder he used a recorder. It was so much easier and he had someone typing it up for him.

How stupid could Mae be? His charm. That kiss. All to what? Keep the investigation livelier? Keep her believing Troy was innocent? For fun and giggles?

She wasn't buying that garbage anymore. She stomped back to the cubicle and collected her things. No longer able to stay here and look him in the eye, Mae needed space to gather her thoughts.

Storming from the SO, she didn't look back.

"Mae! Mae!" Cash called as she stalked across the lot to her car. Now was not the time. "Wait. Where are you going? Did you get a call?"

She spun around, anger simmering on her tongue, white hot. "Yeah, a wake-up call. I don't consider myself a schoolgirl. I never have but I've confirmed to myself that clearly I am shallow enough to be captured by masculine appeal."

Cash's brow furrowed. "What are you talking about?"

"I'm an investigator for crying out loud. I'm supposed to read people and see through deception, yet I've proven what a joke I am." She hated herself for allowing tears to erupt. She was tougher and stronger than this but she was hurt and fuming.

Cash inched forward. "Mae, you've lost me."

"I never had you. All your allure and your talk about faith and change. I fell for it. *Again.* I believed there was something good in you and about you. I let you in. Let you be my first kiss!"

Cash's eyes widened and his mouth slipped open.

"And against my better judgment, I work with you and let you dupe me all over again. Kiss me all over again. For what? You haven't changed. You're still taking advantage of women and using that face and those buttery words to do it."

Hurt registered in his eyes and he held up a hand. "I have changed. I'm not duping you or anyone into anything. What would be the endgame?" He invaded her personal space and she couldn't make herself step back. "And," he said in a lowered voice as he tenderly lifted her chin, "I didn't know I was your first kiss."

"Yeah, well." She pulled away. "I saw you flirting

with Teri and getting her to do the worst part of this job. Your reports. I saw how you manipulated her. And she lapped it up like a puppy. What favor are you gonna do? I have a good idea."

He ground his jaw and his nostrils flared. "I see." He nodded once. "Well, if that's how you feel. I guess we know where we stand with one another. I've got a case to work." He spun and headed back to the SO without so much as a weak excuse or flimsy lie.

Cash stumbled inside, reeling. After everything he'd done to prove how sorry he was and how much he'd changed, all Mae saw was the same troubled boy from the past. She'd hammered him with her words and ill thoughts and splintered him right there in the parking lot.

Teri rounded the corner. "Hey, I have a…" The words died on her lips. "What's going on?"

He leaned his head back against the wall and closed his eyes. "Mae overheard our conversation. Took it out of contest."

"Context, bud," Teri said. "Did you set her straight? Tell her that you have dyslexia and I'm helping you out."

"No. Because maybe this is for the best."

Teri huffed. "You are so into her. It's obvious. Why would this be for the best?" She held up her hand and shook her head. "Is this the whole 'you can't be with someone because you have dyslexia' thing?"

"It's not about *me* having it. It's about children inheriting it, and there's a heavy chance they could. I've unintentionally led her on by allowing my feelings to lead me rather than my head. Now…it's fixed." He raked a hand through his hair.

"Cash Ryland, this is far from fixed. You need to tell her the truth. Tell her why I help you and how you're helping me. If for nothing else, rescue *my* reputation."

He could simply tell Mae about the dyslexia and why he couldn't be with her even though he wanted to. That would be the adult thing to do. But he was a coward. "Even if I did tell her. Even if the whole kid thing was worked out, she doesn't *believe* me. How can two people have an intimate relationship without trust? She's constantly watching and waiting for the shoe to drop because she believes there's a shoe."

"I wish I could whack you with a shoe and her too. You both have junk to work through, but letting her believe lies isn't honorable or noble. So you know." She sighed and left him alone with the dull ache growing inside him.

He couldn't fix anything at the moment but he could work the case. Think outside the box.

Mae walked into the hospital and climbed the stairs to Grandma Rose's new room. She'd been transferred to the step-down unit and could have visitors more often.

She lightly knocked and entered the sterile room, the smell of bleach and antiseptic clinging to the chilly air. Grandma Rose was covered with white blankets—as white as her short hair that was flatter in the back due to days of lying in a hospital bed. She'd want to have it set as soon as she could get out of here.

"Grandma Rose," Mae whispered in case her grandmother was sleeping, but her wrinkled lids opened and her soft gray eyes met Mae's.

"Well, aren't you a sight to see." Grandma Rose

shifted and bumped the bed tray that held a foam glass of water and her Bible.

She didn't feel like a sight to see. She adjusted the tray for Grandma Rose, then perched on the side of her bed. "You warm enough? It's cold in here to me."

"I'm fine. Why are you so glum?"

Mae sighed and toyed with the edge of the blanket.

"You remember Cash Ryland? The guy that stole my essay?" She'd cried to Grandma Rose about it. Mom hadn't said much other than she was sorry and Dad told her to take the bad with the good and move forward.

"I most certainly do. I remember because he'd never had a gingersnap and ate nearly the entire tray before apologizing that time you studied at my house." She chuckled. "My, but he was a looker."

Even Grandma Rose wasn't blind to it and she had cataracts.

"Well, he's a detective with the sheriff's office and I've been working a case with him." She spilled her guts. Grandma Rose had always been her safe place and voice of reason. All that was missing was a glass of milk and oatmeal cookies that were offered in times of trouble.

"Well, it sounds to me like you wanted to see the worst in him to protect yourself from being vulnerable and admitting that you might deeply care for this man."

Had she? "He didn't deny anything I said."

Grandma Rose grasped Mae's hand with both of hers, frail but holding much emotional strength. "Well, honey, you did throw his past in his face. That's not fair fighting."

"But it's true," Mae insisted. Cash had been a hound

and a player. He had manipulated to get whatever he'd wanted or he'd stolen it.

"And how would you feel if God threw your past in your face after forgiving you? Even if it was true."

Lousy. Crushed. Shell-shocked.

She counted on God's mercy but she'd not shown any to Cash whether he was guilty or innocent. Even more so if he was guilty. Mercy was being treated in the opposite way of what one deserved. "Why wouldn't he have at least tried to defend himself?"

A sad laugh bubbled up from Grandma Rose's lips. "You'd already declared him guilty. Would anything he said have mattered or altered your perception?"

No. She'd been expecting and watching for him to make a mistake and confirm he couldn't be trusted. "It's hard to give someone the benefit of the doubt. Sometimes it's even hard to trust God. Men have constantly hurt, betrayed or let me down. Even my father."

"That makes it right to throw every man in the same dog pile? To throw your heavenly father in the dog pile?"

No. But she had.

Grandma Rose cradled her Bible then flipped pages. "I want to read you something. *But this one thing I do, forgetting those things which are behind, and reaching forth unto those things which are before...* Paul wrote that in Philippians."

The backs of Mae's eyes burned. That couldn't be a fluke. "That's the same Scripture the pastor preached from yesterday morning at church. He talked about moving from painful pasts and forgiving those who hurt us so we can move forward in Christ and glorify Him."

"That's good preachin'."

"Why's it have to be so hard?"

Grandma Rose gave one solid hoot. "Age-old question. Life is hard and we have this thing called free will that gives us the ability to choose how we behave." Mae caught the sarcasm and grinned.

"I'm going to tell you something I never told anyone, not even your mama. Fifty-two years ago, a woman married the man of her dreams and on their first anniversary, she discovered he'd had an affair. She ran home to Mama who told her she had two choices. Forgive and press on or divorce him. She wanted to divorce him because going back was too hard and she could no longer trust him. But he begged for a second chance and promised to be faithful. She decided to do the hard thing and stay. Guess what?"

"What?"

"He remained faithful and they rebuilt the trust that had crumbled. Thing about rebuilding—most people don't rebuild a weaker wall or home. They build it better and stronger. That's what we did."

Grandpa Felix had cheated on Grandma Rose? Shock kept her speechless.

"If I hadn't forgiven and moved forward you wouldn't be here. He made a horrific mistake. And I thought I'd die. I really did. But I didn't die. I survived and we made a joyful life. I fought for our marriage. You're a fighter, Mae. Fight the good fight. Keep the faith. Forgive Cash and instead of running away, run right back to him and talk about what you saw. Be an adult about it."

Mae laid her head on Grandma Rose's chest and she stroked her hair like when she was a child. "I'm scared."

"So what? Do it afraid. Chances are he's scared too.

But whether or not you make a go of it, you owe him an apology for throwing his past in his handsome face."

"He does have a great face." She snickered and squeezed Grandma Rose.

"He does, but the important part is truly forgiving and that means no more tossing up his wrongs. I did that often at first with Grandpa. If felt delicious to make him feel so bad, but after that initial high of holding it over his head, I was miserable. Because I wasn't allowing him or *myself* to heal."

Grandpa Felix had always been Mae's favorite. He was kind and generous and no matter where he was or what he was doing, he wore that gold wedding band. One time he'd nearly had his finger cut off when the band got hooked on machinery but now Mae understood the symbolism, the significance of that wedding band and never removing it.

She did need healing. She wanted to be healed. But it felt impossible.

"I love you, Mae."

Oh, how she loved Grandma Rose. After pulling it together, she drove back to the SO. To at least give Cash a chance to explain if he chose to. She parked in a space closest to the back door, her stomach in knots. She texted Cash and asked him to come outside.

He texted back he'd be there in a minute.

She swallowed the lump in her throat and got out of the car in the squelching heat. He made his way to her with wary steps.

"I shouldn't have gone off like I did," Mae said when he reached her. "I'm sorry for that. I'd like to give you the chance to explain." She peered into his eyes. He was still angry. Upset.

He ran his tongue across his top teeth and sighed. "I should have been given that chance right off the bat, Mae. And that tells me all I need to know about what you think of me. So let's just let sleeping dogs lie. Work this case." His voice was strained and he flexed his fingers.

"I tend to think the worst, Cash. I've been hurt a lot."

Cash cupped the back of his neck. "I've been hurt a lot too, Mae. Maybe not in the same ways, but I'm no stranger to pain. To ridicule. Hate. Mistreatment. I've been misunderstood. Betrayed. You're not the only one."

"Can we maybe try again? Go slower?" The fact that she was even voicing this was a huge hurdle. Forget what was behind and reach for what could be.

Cash's face twisted like she'd impaled him on a spike of suffering. "I wish we could. But I think it's best if we don't."

That was fair. She deserved that. She blinked back tears. "Okay," she whispered. "Let's work the case then."

"Okay," he mumbled and trudged inside as she followed behind. Inside, Teri stood near the hallway. Mae watched Cash catch her eye and give his coworker an almost invisible head shake. Teri frowned and disappeared down the hall.

TWELVE

Cash excused himself to the restroom to regroup. Hearing Mae admit she wanted to try again, to move slowly—to have a relationship—were words he'd always imagined her saying. But where would that lead? To more heartbreak. More pain.

He'd appreciated her coming back and asking to hear him out. But she'd already made a quick judgment and in the future what if she continued to make those same kinds of allegations? He could barely stomach all the trouble he'd caused her, caused Troy, caused the people he'd stolen from. He had a mile-high list of sins and guilt. Sins he'd been forgiven for, but forgiving himself was so much harder and he couldn't afford for Mae to sling more mud later on.

He inhaled a few deep breaths and splashed cold water on his face. He met Mae in the conference room where they'd been working. Tension had built a thick and uncomfortable wall, and he wasn't sure how to tear it down or even if he should attempt it.

"Let's take each suspect and rehash what we know about them publicly, privately and if there's anything secretly that we know or can find out." Cash grabbed a dry-erase marker. "Wayne Furlow."

"He's a stand-up guy to the community. Cracks down hard on domestic violence. That clearly showed in Troy's case." Mae flipped through the court transcript. "Was it only Troy's case or is he hard on all men who abuse women? If it's just Troy, then we may have a vendetta of sorts. He's this great defender of the people and Lisa turns him down for a wifebeater? That would stick in his craw. We could run that angle."

He nodded.

Mae picked up her phone. "I wonder how much Wayne donates to the domestic crisis shelter and the hotline." She ran her fingers across the phone keyboard and in a few minutes, he heard a notification. "Lilith says Chancellor Pendergrass told her that he donates about ten grand a year to them. That's significant."

"Can we find out if his mom may have been abused by his father? That could be a reason he's so tough on domestic violence cases and it may help us find a connection if there's one to be found."

Mae scrolled through her computer. "We need to go to the courthouse and either talk to his secretary, if she's willing to help us without his knowledge, or find a deputy clerk at the courthouse with a sharp memory."

"I think we'll have a better shot with a deputy clerk." Cash had seen the way Wayne's young secretary had looked at him, and the way he'd massaged her shoulders. She would be loyal to a fault. Cash grabbed his keys and Mae followed him to his vehicle, keeping a measure of distance between them. The kind of distance that could be felt in every painful breath.

He'd left his workout duffel bag on the passenger

seat. He unlocked the trunk with the intention of tossing the bag there for later when he'd have time to sweat out some of the stress. As he heard the click—

Oh no. No!

"Get down!" He dove out of the way as the lid raised, snagging Mae around the waist and taking her with him. Before he hit the pavement, he tucked her close to his chest so he'd take the brunt of the impact while keeping her protected.

A huge boom broke through the atmosphere and sent a ringing in his ears. Smoke billowed to the sky and flames licked his car. Everyone from inside came charging, weapons drawn. Debris and glass rained down, hot and piercing on Cash's back. He tucked his head, his nose against Mae's throat; her pulse beat against his lips.

"Mac," he rasped. Sirens blared in the distance. Ambulance. Fire trucks. "Are you hurt? Talk to me."

She blinked, soot streaking her face. "What happened?"

"Bomb. Unlocking the trunk triggered it and raising it set it off." Anyone could have done it between Saturday night and today. He hadn't been in his trunk since Saturday morning.

"Everybody alive?" Barrett asked and hovered over Cash and his sister.

"Yeah," Cash said and peered into Mae's eyes, holding them for a moment. He brushed hair from her face and gave her a relieved smile. That's all he had to give.

Barrett helped Cash up and off Mae then inspected his sister as firefighters snuffed out the flames. Cash surveyed the damage and acknowledged his safety to paramedics, colleagues and friends. The bomb didn't do much but blow the trunk and contents inside to bits, leaving the car on fire. The surrounding area hadn't been affected, which meant whoever set it didn't want to do damage to anything other than Cash—and likely Mae.

They'd tow the car and do forensics. Anyone with half a brain and the internet could figure out how to build a bomb.

His cell rang and he glanced at the screen. The prison.

His stomach sank further. Could this day get any worse? He answered. "Detective Ryland."

"Detective Ryland, this is Warden Royce. I'm afraid Troy's gotten an infection—possibly sepsis—from his wounds and he's being transported to the hospital for treatment."

Yes, the day could get worse. Warden Royce wasn't going to tell him which hospital. No point going down that road again. "I see. Please keep me in the loop."

"We will." After a few more words of assurance that Troy would receive the best care, Cash ended the call.

Mae held her arms around her chest and shivered. She was putting up a brave front but he saw the terror in her eyes.

He laid a hand on her shoulder. "It's going to be okay. We'll find who's doing this."

She nodded. "I need to go home and clean up. You need a ride to go do the same?"

He needed to keep her close, but since she was going home to clean up that was pretty much out. If he offered for her brother to escort her, she'd probably punch him.

"I can get another car. Meet you back here in an hour?"

"I'll meet you at the clerk's office."

He nodded and after answering a few more questions, he hurried home to wash the dirt and grime away then he pulled up beside Mae at the county courthouse.

They strode down the hall to the clerk's office. Cash tugged on his ear—everything sounded underwater. The clerk's office smelled of a Mexican lunch and hints of flowery perfume. Evelyn Sheen smiled and waved.

"Hey, Evelyn," he said and introduced Mae.

"I heard about the explosion at the SO. Glad to see you're in one piece—the both of ya. How can I help you?"

"I'm doing some investigating on the down-low," he murmured.

Evelyn leaned in, happy to conspire. "Do tell," she said.

"I need to know if Wayne has tried any homicide cases involving domestic violence."

Evelyn adjusted her purple rhinestone glasses and tapped her lip with unpainted nails. "You know Wayne's sister was in an abusive marriage. He helped her out of it and she's remarried now, living near Hattiesburg, I think. Anyway, I know he put the hammer down on the ex-husband when he was arrested for contributing to the delinquency of a minor—bought a kid beer. Wayne prosecuted. The guy did his eleven months and twenty-nine days in county. I guarantee when he runs for attorney general, domestic violence will be part of his platform."

That helped drive motive. "Any homicide cases?"

"I can do a little digging, but one does stand out because it was four years ago. I remember because my grandbaby was born and I had to leave work. A man in Tate County shot his wife about four months after their divorce was finalized. Wayne made sure to take that case himself. It was really sad. The woman was pregnant. The ex pled not guilty and said they were getting back together. He would never kill her or their child. The child was his. I remember that. Because I was thinking as I held my newborn grandbaby, how could anyone do that?"

Evelyn's mind was a steel trap, mostly because she fed off sad and gruesome cases. She tapped on her keyboard. Most of the cases had been digitalized but they weren't organized by crime. "The gun was his and he had the powder or whatever on his hands. And he'd used his key to get in. Front door was cracked open. No break-in."

"Can you send those files to my email address when you get them. I need any and all of those."

"You got it."

"And if you don't mind—"

"Mum's the word." She pretended to zip her lips and toss away the key. "You think Wayne's doing something illegal?"

"I don't know. Until I do I'd rather him not get wind."

"Done and done." Evelyn saluted and returned her attention to her computer. "I'll send them as I find them."

He thanked her before he and Mae left the building. He'd never tried to fry an egg on pavement, but he had a sneaky feeling today would be the day to prove it could be done. "That case sounds awfully similar to Troy's. Evidence stacked against an ex-husband. Slam-dunk win. The manner of death is different from Lisa's, but that means nothing."

"I'd like to know who the defendant's attorney was."

"Me too."

They drove back to the SO in silence. No word on the bomb or how it was made yet. Inside, Cash checked his email. Evelyn had sent him two more cases making a total of three. "Okay," he said as he pulled up the gunshot case. The letters blurred. "I'm gonna forward them to you so we can both look over them." He found the forward arrow and typed in Mae in the send-to line. Her address popped up and he sent them. Her computer dinged with the notification.

Normally, he'd use his reader program and have the case read through audio. His stomach knotted. *I need to tell her.* Shame overrode his good sense. Mae piped up. "Cash, Harrison Trout was his attorney. When did you say Trout moved here? Five years ago?"

Cash nodded.

"This one appears to be the first case in these three that we have. Drake Halloram was charged with murdering his wife, Betsie. Divorce presided over by Chancellor Sharp. Notes here indicate that she stayed for a short period at the crisis house Chancellor Pendergrass runs. We should ask her about Betsie. Or Lilith might know."

"What about the second case?"

Mae scanned the information, a concentrated expression on her face. "A year later. Bubba Rodham divorced eight months from Leigh White-Rodham. Struck with a crystal vase from their wedding then strangled. Bloody vase was found under his sink cleaned but luminol had revealed traces. No forced entry. He didn't have a key but he professed they were getting back together, and if that's true, then she would have let him in. He pled not guilty. Defense attorney was none other than Harrison

Trout and Wayne Furlow tried the case. That's two for two—or three for three counting Lisa's case."

A pattern was emerging. "What county?"

"Panola. And the third one was in Tate county too. Theresa Chastain. Pushed down the stairs. Divorced about seven months. Same claim. Getting back together. The ex had blood on his shoes and traces of soil from where he lives—on a lake—were found at the landing of the stairs. Another stacked case. According to this, she'd also called local authorities for domestic violence." Mae leaned forward, her elbows on her knees.

"So, we have four women, counting Lisa, who were allegedly murdered by their abusive ex-husbands within a year of their divorce. All the men claimed innocence and that they were getting back together or in the process of working things out. All were tried by Wayne Furlow with serious fury—possibly because of the domestic abuse relating to his personal experience with his sister. Who presided over the other three cases?"

Mae glanced at her screen. "Chancellor Sharp presided over Lisa, Betsie, Theresa. Chancellor Pendergrass presided over Leigh Rodham's. But Chancellor Sharp was senior chancellor, which meant he handled the court caqses and docket."

He could easily have pawned one off on Chancellor Pendergrass as not to raise suspicion in case he was the perpetrator. But he was dead. "Mae, are you seeing a pattern?"

"Oh yeah. We have a possible serial murderer." She blew a heavy breath. "I need to call my unit chief."

Cash's mind whirled. The pattern was too precise for all four of these murders to be coincidences.

A deadly pattern.

The next question was what was the motive behind killing the ex-wife and framing the ex-husband? If a killer wanted to punish an abuser, then why not kill him and call it a day? Unless the killer wanted them to suffer for what they did. Putting them in prison would be utter misery, especially when they knew they were innocent. But why kill the wife? A cruel means to an end? That didn't make sense. But then, killers had warped views and many times their reasoning was twisted.

The upside was Troy may be closer to freedom—if he made it through the woods concerning his infection.

"Leave it to you to stumble upon a serial killer," Colt said. Mae grinned over the phone at her unit chief.

"Right? I'll keep you updated."

"Everything else going okay?"

Minus almost being blown to smithereens and Cash rejecting her hopes of a second chance. Sure. "Yep." The truth was that Cash was right. Deep down Mae still had mistrust issues concerning him. How did one completely give her heart to someone she couldn't trust— even if she wanted to? No room left in her brain to think about it. Right now, they had a possible serial killer loose in the neighboring counties and chances were the killer was someone within the judicial system.

She pocketed her phone and met Cash at the vending machine into which she plunked in her coins for a soft drink and a pack of Nabs. "Whoever killed these women had to know about the abuse and divorces, and they had enough knowledge to frame the exes."

"I think we have to rule out Judge Sharp. He may have had information that could have led us to the real killer and that's why he was killed. To keep us from

discovering the serial murders, and the killer himself."
Cash hit the button and a bottle of water clinked and
clanked then fell to the bottom of the machine. He retrieved it and opened it while she unwrapped her crack-
ers.

"The only suspect that makes sense is Wayne Furlow.
He has a serious beef with men who commit domestic violence. Can we connect any of the other victims
to Wayne? Personally. We know we can connect him
through the criminal court system."

"We can give it a try. We also need to try to connect Trout to the victims prior to their murders. If he
stalked them, was rejected and then murdered them and
framed the ex-husbands to throw off the law's scent
toward him, then that makes even more sense. Wayne
has no allegations or restraining orders against him."

Mae rolled the thoughts around in her head. "It's
got to do with the domestic violence...or maybe the
divorce?"

"A killer targeting divorced couples, killing the
women and framing the men. Why?" Cash asked.

"I don't know. Feels like we're chasing wind. They
aren't targeted according to looks or age. Abuse or divorce is the common thread."

Returning to the victimology, Mae agreed to follow social media leads while Cash made phone calls to
friends and family of the previous victims. She checked
the first victim's social media. Sometimes loved ones
left their profiles active as memorial pages where people could post fond memories or pictures. Betsie's was
open. She clicked on the photos section and scrolled
through the ones made public, which were most. Each
uploaded photo came with an update status and date it

was written. She worked her way down to the year and months prior to Betsie's murder.

Anything at all to do with Harrison Trout? No pictures. She then went to her wall and scrolled down for posts that might mention him around the time prior to her murder. It was going to take a while since it was four years ago.

Cash hung up the phone. "Theresa Chastain worked as a hygienist for a dentist in town. I'm going to call and ask if they remember Harrison Trout coming in for a cleaning or anything that might connect them."

"Betsie posted often so it's taking longer." As she continued to search the victim's posts, Cash talked with the receptionist at the dental office. Mae found nothing other than Betsie mentioned dating a younger man. Some comments were funny, mostly congratulatory. She didn't mention a name and there were no photos of her with him, but the relationship banner had been marked.

Who was this man? Harrison Trout was older than Betsie.

A comment jumped out.

You deserve to be happy with your lawman! Congrats.

Betsie had been dating a younger lawman. Police officer? Deputy? The friend's name was Shakendra Robbins. Mae clicked on her profile. Hopefully, she was smart enough not to publicize her number under her profile information. No number. Good.

Cash hung up the phone. "We might have a break. Trout was one of Theresa's clients. She shined those pearly whites every six months like clockwork."

"Betsie was dating a younger officer around the time she died."

Cash gaped. "Theresa too. The receptionist said it was short-lived. They broke up a few weeks before she was killed. According to her, Theresa was private about her new man but the receptionist said she told her he had the bluest eyes and deepest dimples." He rolled his eyes. "She thinks he was a deputy. Newbie."

There were now more questions than answers. "I'm going to contact this Shakendra Robbins. See if she remembers who this lawman was." She called Dispatch and had them pull up Shakendra's number then she called it.

"Hello."

"Hi, Shakendra Robbins?"

"Yes," she said with wariness in her tone.

"This is Agent Mae Vogel with the Mississippi Bureau of Investigation cold case unit. I'm working on a case that's led me to Betsie."

"Okay."

"Do you know the lawman that Betsie was dating?"

"Ooh. Blue Eyes. She wouldn't give up a name because he was working his way out of a sticky relationship and didn't want to go public until it was officially over. But, I saw him once in his sheriff's car. Real blond like lemonade."

The guy was a player, a lady's man or he was lying to protect his name so he could kill them later. Billy Anderson had blond hair and blue eyes. He was in his late twenties or early thirties she'd guess. And he didn't know when to back off. Lauren had recently been divorced. Mae's stomach roiled. She'd call her and warn her to be extra cautious. She didn't want to further scare her, but she wanted her to be more alert just in case.

"Anything else you can tell me?" Mae asked.

"No. She broke things off with him and it wasn't long after Drake killed her." Or the deputy did.

She thanked her and hung up. "We have a younger deputy dating women and wanting it to stay private. Why? Can we link Harrison on a more personal level to the victims?"

After two hours of work, they'd connected Harrison Trout to all four victims, but they'd only connected the mystery deputy to Betsie and Theresa. But they were still searching.

Exhausted, Mae rubbed her neck and checked her watch. It was late.

"I'm gonna talk to Lisa's best friend, Holly, again," Cash said.

The last time they talked, they'd questioned her about Harrison Trout or anyone who might have bothered her. When Lisa died three years ago, Holly had told police Lisa hadn't dated anyone, but she was certain Troy had murdered her. Now with new evidence she may divulge info she hadn't then.

Cash gave her a thumbs-up with the phone to his ear then his face blanched. "I see. Are you sure?" His jaw twitched. "Thanks." He hung up.

"What'd she say?"

"She held back information because she wanted to see Troy go down for the murder. Plus, she never believed anyone else was guilty."

"Who was she seeing? Was it Billy Anderson?"

Cash pinched the bridge of his nose. "No. She was seeing your brother."

THIRTEEN

Mae walked into Grandma Rose's house, her entire body numb. Barrett. Light blond hair like Mae's. Blue eyes that had always mesmerized girls, and dimples. When asked about Lisa, he'd been short and irritated.

Mae had let it go because he was her brother. But after faxing over a photo of Barrett to Shakendra there was no denying who the younger mystery boyfriend was. She'd positively identified him. Barrett was connected to at least three of the four victims—and possibly all of them.

Mae strode into the kitchen to make tea and regroup and try to make sense of the fact that Barrett was on her suspect list.

Mae and Cash agreed they needed to take a break and would resume tomorrow. They'd talk to Barrett together. But she couldn't let it go and called Barrett's cell phone, getting voice mail. "Hey, it's Mae. I need you to call me when you get this message. I know." She ended the call.

She put a kettle of water onto the stove and dropped a spearmint tea bag in a chipped white mug then turned on the TV for background noise. When the tea whistle blew, she turned off the burner and poured boiling water over the bag, the smell of spearmint enveloping her senses.

A furious pounding on the front door jolted her, and she saw Barrett's cruiser in her driveway.

Fine. They'd do this face-to-face.

She opened the door to icy eyes, a set jaw and flared nostrils. "What do you think you know, Mae?" Barrett demanded then pushed past her into the house. She closed the door and braced herself.

"I know about Betsie, Theresa…Lisa. Do I need to go on?"

"What about them?"

Was he serious right now? "Don't play stupid. I know you dated them. Explain." She folded her arms over her chest and waited. Shock hit her system as she watched him think, calculate and search for a way to lie. Dread formed an icy ball in her stomach.

Moments later he shrugged, but his eyes were hard. "Last I checked dating wasn't a crime."

"That's how you're gonna play this? I can connect you to three out of four murder victims just weeks prior to their deaths. And you didn't want them to tell anyone about you. Explain that, hotshot."

"Have you ever thought I might be dating multiple women and didn't want the talk out? Not that I expected it to stay silent. Women can't keep their mouths shut."

Mae blinked a few times. "You sound like Dad. And a killer."

He took a step toward her and she retreated. While she'd never been afraid of Barrett, right now she was.

"You better watch your mouth, Mae."

"Why? Afraid I'll do the womanly thing and tell the town you're the number one suspect."

His smug grin sent shivers along her spine. "Tell whoever you want. No one will believe you, Mae. They never have."

She shrank back. He was right. No one had believed her about the bullying on the playground, the underwear, the essay. No one had believed Lauren when she'd been assaulted. No one would believe this either. Her insides wilted. She had no clear evidence to prove Barrett murdered those women.

And he clearly relished taunting her with her past.

At her loss for words as the shame and anger of her past reeled through her system, Barrett sidestepped her.

"That's what I thought." He left the house with the door hanging wide open. The phone rang.

She couldn't move. Couldn't think.

Lauren. She answered on autopilot.

"Mae, I think I need help. I got a gift box with a dead rat inside! A dark car keeps driving by. I'm scared."

"Lock your doors. Text me your address. I'm on my way." She grabbed her purse and her gun, locked up and glanced at her text. Elmwood subdivision.

In fifteen minutes, she arrived at Lauren's. The nasty dead rat lay on the stoop with its head cut off. She grimaced and took photos then knocked. "It's me," she hollered and the locks clicked. Lauren opened up, her face pale and eyes wide. "Billy's tried to call me for the past couple of days but I've been ignoring them after your warning to be extra careful. Today was my off day and I spent it with my mom. I got home…" She pointed to the door through tears. "What does that mean?"

Mae wasn't sure. "Do you have anywhere you can go to feel safe?"

"Not anywhere he can't find me."

Sadly, Lauren wouldn't be safe with Mae because she'd become a target by her own brother, but Mae had nothing to arrest him on. Nausea swept over her. "I know a place. It's a safe house for women who've been abused."

"I know about it. I've called the hotline, and after talking with someone a few times, I left Robbie."

"Oh. Oh good." Lauren couldn't seem to catch a break and Mae's heart ached for her. She found Lilith's number and hit the call button. Her friend answered on the third ring.

"Hey, Mae. What's up?"

"I need a favor. I'm with Lauren Jenkins. She's being stalked by an old boyfriend. I'll be up-front with you—it's Billy Anderson."

"*Deputy* Anderson? For real?" Lilith's skepticism seeped through the line.

"Yeah. Long story. But tonight, he left her a dead rat with a severed head as a gift. She's not returning his calls and I had words with him a few days ago."

"Doesn't look like it did anything but make him madder. How can I help? You want me to say something to him?"

"No. I need a place for Lauren to stay for a few days. Is there room at the safe house?" *Lord, please let there be room.*

Lilith's groan said it all. There was no room for Lauren. Maybe she could put her up in a hotel. "No. We're full. But the second house we're remodeling has running water and electricity and at least two bedrooms that will suffice. I wouldn't call it luxury or anything but she's welcome to stay. I'll meet you out there." She gave her the address. "It's out past Fogg Road."

"I know where you're talking about." Out in the country. Secluded. Perfect. She ended the call and told Lauren to pack a bag for a few days and to hurry. Lauren was in the living room and ready to go in ten minutes and shaking uncontrollably.

"Hey," Mae said in a calming tone. "I promise you'll be safe." She hadn't been safe in college. Not in her marriage. Not when she tried to start over by picking a man who had sworn to protect. But Mae meant every word. She would not let Lauren be hurt again. "I've watched while you were packing and no one drove by but my car's outside so he may be laying low. Let's move quickly, okay?" She drew her weapon and let Lauren lock the door then they hurried to the car. Mae opened the passenger door and kept an eye on the road. Once Lauren was in, Mae jumped in the driver's side and backed out.

After circling the block and driving through a neighboring subdivision, she hopped on Highway 51 confident they weren't being followed.

Lauren wrung her hands in her lap. "I never thought I'd be here, you know?"

"I know."

"I just wanted to go to college, have fun, learn to be a nurse and get married and have kids and a career. But things went so wrong." Lauren sniffed and Mae dug a tissue from the console and passed it to her then held her hand. Sometimes not saying anything was wiser than trying to find the right platitude.

Mae maneuvered Fogg Road's winding curves.

Kudzu framed the road from the ground to the tops of the trees like a plague overtaking nature. Watching closely, she spotted the hidden road—nothing but dirt and gravel—that led up and around to the two-story 1950s farmhouse with peeling paint and a sagging roof.

She parked behind Lilith's marked unit and hurried up to the front door with Lauren in tow. Lilith welcomed them inside. "It's a project but it'll be a great place when it's done. We're working off donations." She had dressed in a Mississippi State T-shirt and a pair of jeans. Her hair was in two tight French braids that ran to her shoulders.

Lilith led them into the kitchen. "One thing we do have that's working is the teakettle. Can I make you a cup of chamomile?"

Lauren nodded and Mae surveyed the old farmhouse. Original hardwood flooring. Bricked wood burning fireplace. Great bones. It just needed some paint and special touches. A couch and two chairs filled the living room. No TV. The kitchen was small and fresh paint smacked her senses. The cabinets had been recently painted white. They shone like new.

"We have two bedrooms downstairs that are livable and four upstairs that need help," Lilith said as she worked to make tea. When it was ready, Mae declined a cup.

"Would you mind if I take it in the bedroom? I'd like a chance to settle in," Lauren said.

"Of course." Lilith pointed down the hall. "First door on the right. It's the bigger bedroom. Bathroom is directly across from you." Lauren thanked her and carried her tea and duffel bag out of the kitchen.

"No tea. How about coffee? You look tired."

"I am tired. It's been a real shoddy day." She rested her arms on the table then laid her head on her arm as a pillow. "This case is killing me."

"Why? Because it's tracking back to Troy?" The smell of coffee grounds permeated the air as well as Lilith's question.

Mae raised her head. "Honestly? Because it's tracking to my brother."

Lilith's eyes widened and she froze with the coffee scoop in midair. "No, it's not."

"Yes, it is. But I can't prove it." She sighed. "Can I admit something too?"

Lilith nodded.

"I can't believe he could do it and—" she lowered her voice "—yet part of me absolutely can. He's always gotten angry when he didn't get what he wanted because he almost always did. He's known to be a hothead. He's definitely got skills and knowledge to plant evidence. He dated at least three of the victims."

"Wait? What? Back up the bus. I thought you were here about Lisa?" She finished loading the filter with grounds and poured in the water then hit the button.

Mae unloaded on Lilith as if she were calling an anonymous hotline. "What's your professional opinion?"

"Man, Mae. I can't believe it's Barrett. He's a little cocky, I'll give you that. But a killer? I don't know. No wonder you're exhausted. My brain is drained from listening." The coffeepot beeped and she poured them two cups. "All I have is cream and sugar."

"Black." Mae accepted her cup and sipped the strong brew. "Good."

"Thanks. That's about the only thing I learned from

my mother." She shook her head and sadness sent her mouth into a downcast position. Mae knew she'd had it rough and that her mother had died.

"She'd gone back to my dad off and on over the years. One night the hits came, like they always had, but this night he hit too long and too hard and she... she didn't make it. I ran across the street to the neighbors and they called the police. I'd come in from working and she was on the floor and Dad was passed out on the couch."

"I'm so sorry, Lilith." Mae squeezed her hand.

Mae couldn't imagine the horrors Lilith had seen and endured. Mae's dad was a piece of work and held double standards, but he'd never put his hands on any of them and she knew he loved Mom. Quiet and easy to fit into the mold he wanted her to fit into. Mae? Not so much. And their heads butted more than two billy goats. The sound of wheels on gravel pulled her attention from her thoughts. "Are you expecting anyone?"

Lilith's eyes narrowed. "No."

Then who was here?

Cash listened as his software played the reports back to him and he audio recorded important details. Four female victims in the past five years. Four men might be wrongly imprisoned.

But why? He needed a savvy profiler and he happened to know one. Two years ago, he'd met FBI agent Chelscy Banks at a cold case conference in North Carolina. He'd gone on his own dime, taking vacation time for the trip. Anything to gain insight and help him prove Troy's innocence.

They'd bumped into one another in the hotel lobby

and hit it off. Once Cash was sure she didn't want anything more than friendship, they'd kept in touch. Maybe she wouldn't be too busy to help him out.

He hit the call button.

"Agent Chelsey Banks," she said. Did she get a new phone? "Just kidding, Cash. I know it's you," she said through a throaty laugh. "Were you worried I ghosted you? Deleted your number?"

He smirked. "No."

"Miss my voice, do ya?"

That earned her a chuckle. "I'm working on a case."

"Your brother's? You getting any headway?" she asked, all joking aside.

"I think so." He briefly gave her the bullet points of the case since the Fourth of July and what he and Mae had stumbled upon with the other victims. "I was wondering if you could help me with a profile. Or something to point me in the right direction."

She low whistled. "Well, I normally need more time and case files in front of my nose to build a solid profile. But I can spitball some ideas that might spark your own profile. I'd have you send me the digital files but to be honest, I'm eyeball deep in a major case right now and stretched thin."

Making an even bigger name for herself in the FBI. Chelsey was ambitious.

"Anything you might throw at me, I'm grateful for." He needed a win and fast.

Chelsey clicked her tongue, like time was ticking at a warp speed. *Tock tock tock tock tock.*

"A bat killed your sister-in-law. A push down the stairs. Gunshot. Strangulation. Give them to me in order."

"Gunshot—"

"Was the husband into guns?"

"Yeah. He was. A hunter and spent time at the range."

"That would make sense for her manner of death. Second?"

"A push down the stairs. And I see where you're going. She'd been at the hospital before for injuries consistent with being shoved down stairs."

"Did she admit that to the medical staff who treated her?"

Cash replayed the audio report in his mind. He'd become an excellent listener. "No. It was noted by the attending ER physician, and after she died they subpoenaed her medical records and saw the doc's speculations."

"Hmm... Third?"

"Strangulation. No defensive wounds. The bungee cord used was the same kind to tie down tarps and they found it with her DNA and a partial print on the metal hook buried under some life vests on his boat."

"Fourth was the beating with a bat—Troy's case. He played ball for his employer on a work league." She had a sharp memory. "Someone knows details about the men and is using those details. The one that stands out most—"

"Is the trip down the stairs. If medical personnel only speculated and it was confirmed after she died, then someone with prior personal knowledge knew to murder her in that manner. Did she confide in one of our suspects? That wouldn't fit Trout. If he were stalking there wouldn't be intimacy. Unless they did date and it came out but then she decided to go back to the ex."

Chelsey crunched into something. Probably ice.

She'd admitted to being addicted to chomping on it while thinking through cases. "The going back to the ex-husband sets off the killer—that's the trigger. A man who sees himself as a worthy love interest would be furious if she were willing to go back to an abuser when he could be her entire world. Of course, he's got a warped view but most killers do. The fact that both suspects are attorneys fits. They like order. They like to be able to showboat and litigating would do that, making them feel important and worthy. There would be a measure of arrogance. Interesting that they're on opposite sides of the judicial system."

Cash agreed. "But would the victims have confided in either of them so quickly? I'd think that wouldn't be the topic of discussion until a relationship turned serious. And the two victims who filed complaints as well as the woman in Louisiana never dated Trout, at least not exclusively in Tamera Smith's case. It was like he saw them, greeted them and became fixated. If Wayne is our guy, he's a public figure and I doubt he'd be able to hide a relationship for any length of time. Plus, he enjoys playing the field and no one has ever complained about him. Not even Lisa."

Chelsey resumed crunching. "True. But she would tell her divorce lawyer upon initial meeting."

"Fitz Leeman came up clean and had an alibi for Lisa's murder, but killers have been known to fake alibis."

"Take another look at him. I'll chew on it and call if something springs to mind."

Cash thanked her and ended the call. Looked like he'd take a ride out and talk to Fitz Leeman again. Then he'd see if Mae had her second wind and wanted to talk shop with some of the ideas that Chelsey had given.

As he grabbed his recorder another thought struck him.

No. That was barking up the wrong tree, but his gut warned him to follow up. He had a stop to make before riding out to the divorce attorney's home.

FOURTEEN

"Lauren!" Mae called as a dark sedan pulled up into the drive. The windows were tinted and she was unable to tell who was driving but Lauren had mentioned a dark sedan. Lauren came into the living room. "What does Billy Anderson drive?"

"Not a car," Lilith said and held her gun to her side as she peeped out the curtain into the front yard at the car. No one got out. "He owns a blue S-10."

"But Billy has been stalking you right?" Mae asked.

"Well…I mean I assumed it was him," Lauren admitted with a red face.

Mae spun on her. "Can you be clearer?"

"He sent me flowers twice with a card at work saying he was sorry and wanted to try again. Then when I told him no, they stopped and a week later resumed anonymously to the hospital and my house. I thought maybe he wasn't signing them anymore because he knew I'd know they were from him."

"Did he try to call you during this time?"

"No."

"But he has tried to call you the past few days?" After Mae had given him the what for. If Billy hadn't been sending her the gifts, he may have been calling to find out why she was telling Mae he was. Or to find out who was.

"Yes. And that is the car that was driving past my house." Lauren tucked her thumbnail between her teeth. "Who is it?"

"I'm about to find out." Mae unholstered her gun and turned the knob, but Lilith held up her hand.

"You take Lauren to the back of the house." She leaned in. "She's comfortable with you and if this goes sideways…"

Mae glanced at Lauren as she trembled against the wall. "Okay. You're right. But if you need backup, leave the front door open and holler. I'll be ready." She clasped Lauren's hand and led her down the hall.

Lauren glanced behind her and gasped. "I know him. His office is next to my divorce attorney's. He asked me out a couple of times, but I turned him down."

Harrison Trout! How on earth would he have found them here? Mae was careful not to be followed. She hadn't noticed him once. Was she losing her A-game? She reached into her back pocket to call Cash but she'd left her phone on the kitchen table.

She heard Lilith's strong, firm voice. "I said back away."

Mae rushed Lauren into the bedroom and shoved her into the closet. "Don't come out no matter what until I come and get you. No matter what you hear or how long it takes. Do you understand?"

Lauren nodded.

Mae tiptoed down the hall as the sound of gunshots echoed through the house, then she sprinted.

She darted into the living room and out the front

door to see Lilith kneeling beside Harrison Trout, her fingers checking for a pulse.

"What happened?"

Lilith peered up at her and shook her head. "He demanded to see Lauren. I said no and to leave or I'd arrest him for trespassing. He pulled a gun. Said he was here to rescue Lauren like he'd tried to rescue the others." She frowned. "What does that mean, Mae?"

"I don't know." Trout held a gun in his limp hand.

"He aimed and I fired first. Three rounds."

Had Trout inadvertently admitted to murdering all four victims? "Did he say how he knew to get here? I'm sure we weren't followed."

"I guess you weren't that sure, Mae. Here he is." She pointed to the now deceased attorney.

"We need to call it in."

"I will." Lilith stood. "You call Cash. Let him know you're okay and where you are. And that you've probably solved the case, though I'm not sure how you'll be able to prove it unless there's evidence at his place. This will get a warrant, though." Lilith frowned. "So much for keeping this place anonymous."

Mae trudged inside and got her phone off the kitchen table. Cash had already tried her three times. She called him back.

"Mae! You scared me half to death. I went by your place and saw you were gone. I called Barrett and he let me know with a serious attitude what went down at your place. I have news."

"So do I. Harrison Trout is dead. Lilith just shot him."

"Lilith? You're with Lilith?"

"Yeah."

"Get out of there. Now! I'll explain later."

Lilith entered the kitchen with the gun aimed on Mae. "Tell Cash to come and get our statements, assess the scene and not to call in backup. I'd hate for the body count to rise before he gets here."

Lilith? Lilith had committed these crimes? Lilith had targeted Cash and Mae?

She'd been right under her nose, but Mae hadn't seen it because she'd been dead set that it must have been a man. Her muscular build... She'd blamed her own brother! "Cash, Harrison Trout is dead and you need to come out and take a statement and come alone, okay?" She gave him the address.

"I understand, Mae. Be careful. I'm coming."

Lilith motioned her chin at the phone. "Hang up. Now."

Mae ended the call.

"Don't even think about grabbing that gun."

She'd set it on the table to make the call.

"Toss the phone down the garbage disposal. Now." Lilith moved forward and retrieved Mae's gun, pocketing it in her waistband.

Mae inched backward and tossed the phone. She had Lauren to think about. *Lord, please don't let her come out of hiding.* "You called Harrison here, didn't you?" Mae was positive she hadn't been followed. "How did you know Harrison was the one stalking Lauren?"

"I know it wasn't Billy and when you told me about the car, I put it together. Harrison is a creep. Everyone knows that. Once you explained you had linked three more cases, I knew it was only a matter of time until you connected the dots."

Lilith? Mae was still stunned.

"Why couldn't you let it go? Troy Ryland is a scumbag who deserved prison time. Just like those other pieces of trash deserved it."

Mae agreed that Troy and any man who hit women deserved punishment by the proper authorities. "What did Betsie, Theresa, Leigh and Lisa do to deserve their brutal deaths, Lilith? Explain that."

"Isn't it obvious?" she asked as if Mae were an idiot. "They were going to go back. After all the hours I'd spent on the hotline phone with them. It's supposed to be anonymous but after many calls it becomes personal. They meant something to me. And after the time I spent with Betsie and Lisa in person. They were going to go back."

Lilith had been in the courtroom during the divorces or aware of them and had personal connections through the hotline.

"Just like my mom went back. And every time she dragged me back with her. She got beat. So did I. Each time was worse until it ended in murder. At least my dad went to prison. Can you imagine if those women had children with these monsters? I couldn't let that happen."

Mae stood appalled as Lilith's eyes filled with tears. "I still have scars on my back. And even more inside. And I couldn't let children be born into that. I just couldn't."

While Mae's tender side hurt with Lilith for the horrific abuse on many levels she'd endured those first eighteen years of her life, it didn't give her the right to take matters into her own hands.

"You understand, Mae. Right? Men, they take and abuse and use women to get what they want. You said that yourself. Of all people, you should get it." Lilith searched her eyes, silently pleading for her to understand.

Mae didn't want to end up like Lilith, in a place where bitterness blurred sound judgment and hate justified crime. Grandma Rose's words slid into her soul. *Forgive.*

Lilith had never forgiven and that hate had grown like thorns around her heart until it twisted her mind to murder.

Cash's words that not all men took advantage, hurt and betrayed rolled into her heart with a soft thud.

"We can blame all this on Harrison. He's a sicko. Stalkers escalate and it would only be a matter of time before he assaulted or murdered one of his victims. Even if he didn't, he terrorizes women. Look at Lauren. She's hiding right now because of him. All we have to say is that Harrison tried to take her. I did my job. You and I protected her. We protected women."

Not like this. "And the innocent men in prison?"

"They aren't innocent!" Lilith hollered. "They deserve to rot there."

Mae calculated her options. Lilith wasn't above killing her. She'd killed four other women. "Did you kill Chancellor Sharp?"

"Sheila wasn't going to leave him. They already had kids but I needed Cash to be busy and less concerned about Troy's case. I thought getting word to Tommy Leonard would end it."

"Your name isn't on the logs. How did you get to him and convince him?"

"Money still talks, Mae. He has a kid. And I know an inmate who got him word for the right price." Her name was on the logs then. Just not on any connected to Tommy Leonard.

Even if she went along with Lilith's insane story, Cash never would and Lilith had to know that.

She did know.

Mae's fear level ramped and everything inside her quaked. Lilith was luring Cash here to shoot him with the gun that she'd planted in Harrison's hand. She'd say Harrison killed Cash and Lilith killed Harrison. Mae could go along with the sick story or be a casualty, and if Lauren stayed put she would be none the wiser, but if she did happen to stumble upon the staging, she'd die in the crosshairs.

"He should be here anytime. I hope you make the right decision."

Mae swallowed hard.

There was only one right choice but no matter what she decided, there would be bloodshed.

Cash's agitation and antsy fear set his nerves crawling under his skin. After talking to Chelsey, she'd made a point that an abused woman would confide in her lawyer. But she'd also confide in another woman. The killer had access to information, basic forensic knowledge and Judge Vickie Pendergrass was tall and fit. She had access to these women and to pertinent information. And a beef with Judge Sharp.

Cash's suspicions sent him to talk with the chancellor but on his way there it hit him that the judge probably wouldn't have known he was looking into Troy's case or that he would be at the Fourth of July celebration as extra security. She also wouldn't have known he'd had Troy's case file at home.

Someone on the inside of the SO would.

Could have been Barrett or even Billy but more likely the unidentified subject would be a woman. He'd called Chelsey again and ran it by her. She agreed. It would likely be a woman who had also been physically abused by a man—husband, boyfriend, father. Someone who had knowledge the ex-husbands were reconciling with their former wives. The unsub would be a woman who wanted to thwart that and see justice served. Lilith Freedman had fit the bill.

As he traveled Fogg Road, every scenario of a coming standoff played out ending with one or all of them dead.

Cash spotted the hidden entrance but bypassed it in case Lilith had video cameras stationed. All Cash had going for him was a surprise attack and a lot of prayer. Parking on the shoulder of the road, he observed his options. All slim. A stretch of land smothered in thick, tangled kudzu. Snakes. Critters. Logs. He was going in blind.

But Mae's and Lauren Jenkins's lives were at stake.

Sliding down the hill at the shoulder of the road, his feet snagged on the winding green vines and the sun baked his skin. Fighting through the mass of kudzu, clambering over fallen trees and rustling up fox dens he neared the farmhouse ahead. An old rusty silo and broken-down barn sat about twenty feet out. Soaked in sweat and adrenaline racing, he prayed and pressed on until he approached the back of the house. Crouching into the mass of itchy ground covering, he surveyed the house, the yard.

No sounds except cicadas and the air-conditioning unit fan whirling. Staying low, he rushed to the windows and peeped inside. Kitchen. He tried the door. Locked.

Wooden clothespins had been clipped to a line. He sprinted for it and snagged one of the pins. For once he was thankful he'd been a juvenile delinquent who'd broken and entered far more houses than he'd like to admit. He was an expert at picking locks.

Cash broke it in half and fashioned the metal hinge into a lock picker. Just like riding a bike. The farmhouse would have old locks and they were easier to manipulate.

In about three seconds, Cash had the door unlocked and pushed it open with a gentle touch, hoping it wouldn't squeak. His pulse pounded and his throat had turned as dry as dust.

Voices sounded toward the front of the house.

Mae!

She was alive. Relieved, he listened a moment longer. Mae was talking with Lilith.

As he crept down the hall, a woman stood in the doorway of a bedroom with a lamp in her hand. When she saw Cash, she shrieked.

Lilith hollered. Mae screamed and Cash raised his arms to keep from being bashed by a glass lamp.

"Nobody moves," Lilith commanded and the woman with the lamp froze. Cash looked up and Lilith stood in the hallway with a gun to Mae's head. Fear pulsed in Mae's eyes but she stayed steady.

"Look at you trying to be sneaky. Pick the lock? Should have known your deviant mind would have kicked into gear. Drop the gun or I'll kill her." Lilith's cold eyes held Cash's gaze.

The woman with the lamp gasped and he darted a

glance at her. "Go back inside and close the door," he whispered. "Don't come out."

"Stop!" Lilith hissed. "She's seen too much." Lilith marched forward, using Mae as a shield. "Kick your gun this way. Now."

Cash had no choice. He lowered his weapon and obeyed. Lilith then kicked it into another room and forced Mae to close the door to that room. "Take that extension cord by the fridge and tie Lauren to the kitchen chair. Do it tightly or Mae dies."

"It's okay," he told Lauren. "Trust me."

Lauren shook her head but came to him anyway. Fear drove her to obediently sit in the chair and let him tie her to it.

"I'm a detective and me and Mae are gonna get you out of here. Okay?" he murmured.

She remained silent, trembling.

"Come on, Cash. Outside." Lilith backed toward the front door, waiting on him to pass the room with the gun inside, then she inched onto the porch. "Keep coming."

Once they were outside, he spotted Trout's body and the gun in his hand.

"Now, Mae has a choice to make. She can corroborate my story about Harrison showing up and turning lethal, forcing me to defend us though unable to save you, or she can choose you and nobody but me makes it out. I'm not looking forward to wounding myself for show, but…" Lilith pressed the gun farther into Mae's temple and she winced.

Cash weighed his options. He could go for the gun in Harrison's hand, which Lilith wasn't paying attention to, but she'd see him dip down and he wouldn't have time to grab it before Lilith killed Mae or him.

There was only one option that held a slim chance of his survival.

But would Mae trust him? He needed her cooperation.

"And let's just recap history here," Lilith said. "Cash fooled you into believing he was interested in you, Mae. You said it yourself. He used you for an essay you worked hard on and robbed you of your dream. He's a user, Mae. He wants his brother freed to hurt other women." She gripped Mae tighter. "Think about that before you choose wrong."

Cash inhaled deeply. "She's right, Mae. Go along with Lilith. It's the only way you survive." Just in case he didn't make it he needed her to know the truth. Now with his life on the line it all seemed so stupid and senseless. "When it's all over...I need you to get with Teri and let her give you something. I've been trying to make a wrong right."

Mae's eyes grew wider, fear stronger. Shock. Confusion. "You want me to go along with a lie to live. And you die?" Her voice rose higher with each word. "You don't need to die to make sure I live."

"But I would, Mae. I would die for you. Ten thousand times over." His words clogged in his throat and he wished he could touch her one more time. More than likely he wasn't coming out of this one and he meant every word.

He loved this woman. There was no way this world should go on without the light that was Mae in it. Bringing her here and onto this case was his fault. He wouldn't let it end this way. But he may be able to save them both. If she would trust him.

Tears streaked down her cheeks. "Why? I've done

nothing but question you and think the worst of you. Why would you do that? Why would you willingly lay down your life for me?"

The backs of Cash's eyes stung and he swallowed the mountain of emotion in his throat. "Because I love you, Mae. Now, trust me."

"Okay," she whispered. She held his gaze and he thought he saw something flash in her eyes. "I trust you," she cried. "I forgive you and I trust you."

"Nice. But I don't believe either of you," Lilith said and fired the gun.

Scorching fire ripped through him, knocking him back and stealing his breath. He crumpled to the ground.

FIFTEEN

Mae didn't have time to be shocked, but she was terrified.

Lilith had fired three rounds into Harrison and three into Cash. Oh, Cash! He had fallen in a crumpled heap, lifeless.

Before Lilith had the chance to also kill Mae, she grabbed Lilith's wrist and thrust it upward, hoping she'd fire off that last round. Mae could hopefully subdue Lilith before she had the chance to reload her magazine.

Lilith was strong—that same strength that had invaded her room the night she'd tried to kill Mae.

Gunfire cracked.

She'd done it! Now she could wrestle her down, but Lilith was already on the ground with a bullet wound in her forehead. Mae whipped around. Cash was on a knee, gun in hand. Harrison's hand was empty.

Shock kept her rooted in place. "You—you took three to the chest!"

Cash opened up his button-down shirt. "I had foresight," he said through a wheeze and cough.

Mae rushed to him and dropped to her knees, touching the impressions in his bulletproof vest.

She collapsed into his arms and knocked him onto his backside. He cradled her in his lap as her fear and panic came out in sobs onto his neck. "You're alive." But he could have died. Lilith had executed Chancellor Sharp with a bullet to the head. She was a crack shot and had she fired those rounds into his face… Cash wouldn't be sitting here holding her or rescuing her. He knew there had been a serious chance he could have died.

It wasn't an act.

Cash Ryland would have died for her. Willingly.

She clung to his neck then peppered him with kisses on his cheeks, lips. "Cash, you brilliant, crazy man." Mae gazed into his watery eyes. "I love you." She pressed her lips to his, but he mumbled something against them.

"What?"

"All in good time." He pulled away from her mouth. "But your friend is tied up inside and has no clue we're alive and she's safe." He grinned and gave her one quick smack to the lips. "Go rescue her."

Mae started after her and stopped. "No."

Cash blinked. "It's now my turn to ask. What?"

Mae shook her head. No. She'd been so wrong. And it wasn't until Cash had willingly laid aside his life for hers that the truth absorbed deep inside. Not all men could be lumped into the *taker* category. There were men who were honorable, heroic and kind.

"You go rescue her. She needs to know that she can trust again. That she can take a chance on a man again. Go unbind her because she's been bound a long time— by men and fear. And so have I. But no more." It was time to heal. To trust again. Not only earthly men, but Jesus. He'd willingly laid down his life out of love for her too. No strings attached. Just a hope that one day she would choose Him even while knowing she would mistrust and question Him often.

Cash brushed his knuckles across her cheek. "You are remarkable. And we have a lot to talk about."

With that, he went inside and rescued Lauren. Only God could rescue her heart.

Cash rubbed his hands on his jeans as his nerves twisted his stomach into knots. It had been two days since the shooting and they'd been buried under paperwork, statements and reporters. No time for anything personal.

Until now.

Troy and the other men were being exonerated. Wayne Furlow had moved at lightning speed to make it happen and apologized to the families as well as publicly. He was a flirt but a decent guy.

Cash and Mae had given statements and her cold case unit had come down to be with her and to get their own reports. He was glad she had such a team.

But now he stood outside on the porch of her grandma's house. He had some things he needed to say. Teri was right. Charlie, his mentor, was right. He was hiding in shame about his disability and fear of the future and that wasn't how God wanted him to live.

He was going to put it all out there and let Mae decide but if she was willing to marry a man who could pass on his problem to a child then they'd figure it out.

Cash knocked and Mae opened the door with a mile-wide grin that would light up the darkest of places. It lit up his darkest places. "Hey," he said. "Can I come in?"

"You know you can," she said and opened the door wider. "You just missed Barrett."

He winced. "How did that go?" Her brother had avoided her since she'd declared him a killer.

"I apologized. He yelled at me and then apologized for throwing bad experiences in my past at me. Realized how much he had sounded like our dad—who, by the way, actually hugged me after I almost died and followed it up with *You should see now why you don't belong in law enforcement. You'll get yourself killed next time.* And then he hugged me tighter. I guess in his weird, old, old, old ways he's trying to protect me. I'll never be anything but the weaker sex who needs to be taken care of. But I sort of get it—not agree, but get." She shrugged with a grin. "Also, I told Barrett to quit being a jerk by playing women. It's not right."

"No, it's not."

"I'm sorry for throwing your past at you, Cash."

"I know." He could hardly contain himself. He wanted to pull her into his arms but it wasn't time. Everything had to be out there. "I want to talk to you. About us." He was a ball of jitters.

"Okay," Mae said warily. She invited him to sit on the couch where she decided to perch but he opted to stand. He pulled the rolled-up notebook papers out of his pocket and handed them to her. "What's this?"

"Read it." He couldn't stand to watch and turned around and stared into empty space growing more anxious by the second, knowing she wouldn't be able to read it entirely. His handwriting was too botched.

"A pervasive essay," she muttered. "Wait. A *persuasive* essay. Cash," she murmured.

He could hear the pages swish as she read each one.

A persuasive essay about how Mae Vogel had persuaded him to take a chance on love. How she was everything that made him want to be a better man. Page after page he'd written about her and how he'd fallen in love with her when he was only eighteen. If he'd have died, Teri would have given it to her so she'd know the truth.

Sniffing drew him around. Mae sat with the papers lying on her lap, crying. He wasn't expecting tears and panic hit his gut.

She held up the essay. "You said you'd never make me cry."

"Are you sad?"

She laughed. "No. No, I don't think I've ever been happier." She tossed them on the couch and flooded his space with her soft, lovely presence.

"But the writing…" Had she not noticed the major issue? He expected it.

"You have dyslexia." She cradled his cheek. "That's why you mix up words sometimes, why you use audio recordings…" She sniffed and wiped her eyes. "And why you let Teri type what you've recorded."

Cash nodded. "Sheriff gave me permission and Teri offered. I wasn't charming her. She wants me to spend extra time with her fiancé, who was paralyzed in an ATV accident, to try to show him that disabilities, whether physical or mental, don't mean that you can't live and move on. But I'm the worst person to do that because I've let it hold me back." He laughed as it dawned. Teri had meant to help him see he was no different from her fiancé. By talking to him she hoped Cash would live and move on too. "She also wants me to build a porch onto her house." He grinned at that. "That's what you overheard."

Mae wrapped her arms around his waist. "Why wouldn't you tell me that?"

"I didn't want you to think I wasn't smart. I liked feeling like a genius in your eyes. And—and after you got angry it was easier to let you be that way because there's a heavy percentage that I could pass this to a child. I can't let a kid grow up like I did. Struggling like I did. I know you want a family." He raked his hand over his face.

"Did you know—growing up—that you had dyslexia?"

"No. When I was given the choice of going to jail or working for Charlie after I shoplifted at his corner store, he discovered it and he helped me."

Mae hugged him tighter. "Cash, don't you see? You didn't have parents who could or would help you get the right tools you needed to be successful or who would support you. There may not have been what there is now, like software. And you are a genius. You are so gifted. Look at how you build things and solve cases and help people. You're tenacious and a fighter and those fearless abilities rescued so many people. Saved many lives. If I have a child with you, I'd want them to be exactly like you."

Moisture filled his eyes. "You mean that?"

"Ten thousand times over," she whispered and cradled his face. "We're both fighters and we'll fight for better education and opportunities for our children and they're bound to be fighters too. They'll come by it honest."

"We may be puttin' the cart before the horse here."

He hadn't expected this kind of grace and compassion but he should have—if he hadn't been so afraid and ashamed he'd have seen it. But fear and shame blinded truth. But on the off chance…

Cash knelt and reached into his other back pocket. He pulled out a black velvet box. He opened it to a gold band with a modest round solitaire that he'd purchased yesterday—though there was nothing modest about his love for her. It was exceptional and far grander. "Mae, will you marry me? Make a life with me. Grow old with me. Probably read the paper to me and maybe type up my reports so Teri can have a break." He grinned at that last little joke and Mae giggled. "The commute from here to Batesville's not too bad."

Mae held out her left hand and he placed the ring on her finger. "I would be honored and proud to be your wife. Nothing would make me happier. Except not having to type your reports." She laughed and dropped to her knees and into his arms.

He dipped into a kiss that would have fogged up a bathroom—but better than that, it fogged up his heart.

"I love you," she whispered breathlessly against his lips.

Who'd have ever thought he—Cash Ryland—would be a man who loved words. Maybe not every word, but those three were his favorite. They were written on his heart and he had no trouble reading them.

Not even a little.

* * * * *

*. If you enjoyed this story,
pick up the previous book in
Jessica R. Patch's Cold Case Investigators
miniseries,* Cold Case Takedown.

Available now from Love Inspired Suspense!

Dear Reader,

Mae spent most of her life experiencing a lot of unfair treatment and double standards that developed into a skewed view of men as a whole and a trust issue with God. As she worked through her struggles, and alongside Cash, she realized that she couldn't lump every man into one category—and that included God. Maybe you've been in the same shoes as Mae or one of the victims in this story. Dear One, you are so loved and cherished by God. He can be trusted to heal you and bring wholeness to your life. He won't mishandle your heart. And if you are in an abusive relationship, please seek help—tell a trusted friend, a pastor or a counselor or call the National Domestic Violence Hotline at 1-800-799-SAFE (7233). But don't stay silent.

Please follow me on BookBub: https://www.bookbub.com/profile/jessica-r-patch and visit my website at: www.jessicarpatch.com.

Jessica

Get 4 FREE REWARDS!

We'll send you 2 FREE Books plus 2 FREE Mystery Gifts.

Love Inspired Suspense books showcase how courage and optimism unite in stories of faith and love in the face of danger.

FREE Value Over $20

YES! Please send me 2 FREE Love Inspired Suspense novels and my 2 FREE mystery gifts (gifts are worth about $10 retail). After receiving them, if I don't wish to receive any more books, I can return the shipping statement marked "cancel." If I don't cancel, I will receive 6 brand-new novels every month and be billed just $5.24 each for the regular-print edition or $5.99 each for the larger-print edition in the U.S., or $5.74 each for the regular-print edition or $6.24 each for the larger-print edition in Canada. That's a savings of at least 13% off the cover price. It's quite a bargain! Shipping and handling is just 50¢ per book in the U.S. and $1.25 per book in Canada.* I understand that accepting the 2 free books and gifts places me under no obligation to buy anything. I can always return a shipment and cancel at any time. The free books and gifts are mine to keep no matter what I decide.

Choose one: ☐ **Love Inspired Suspense Regular-Print** (153/353 IDN GNWN)   ☐ **Love Inspired Suspense Larger-Print** (107/307 IDN GNWN)

Name (please print)

Address   Apt. #

City   State/Province   Zip/Postal Code

Email: Please check this box ☐ if you would like to receive newsletters and promotional emails from Harlequin Enterprises ULC and its affiliates. You can unsubscribe anytime.

Mail to the Harlequin Reader Service:
IN U.S.A.: P.O. Box 1341, Buffalo, NY 14240-8531
IN CANADA: P.O. Box 603, Fort Erie, Ontario L2A 5X3

Want to try 2 free books from another series? Call 1-800-873-8635 or visit www.ReaderService.com.

*Terms and prices subject to change without notice. Prices do not include sales taxes, which will be charged (if applicable) based on your state or country of residence. Canadian residents will be charged applicable taxes. Offer not valid in Quebec. This offer is limited to one order per household. Books received may not be as shown. Not valid for current subscribers to Love Inspired Suspense books. All orders subject to approval. Credit or debit balances in a customer's account(s) may be offset by any other outstanding balance owed by or to the customer. Please allow 4 to 6 weeks for delivery. Offer available while quantities last.

Your Privacy—Your information is being collected by Harlequin Enterprises ULC, operating as Harlequin Reader Service. For a complete summary of the information we collect, how we use this information and to whom it is disclosed, please visit our privacy notice located at corporate.harlequin.com/privacy-notice. From time to time we may also exchange your personal information with reputable third parties. If you wish to opt out of this sharing of your personal information, please visit readerservice.com/consumerschoice or call 1-800-873-8635. **Notice to California Residents**—Under California law, you have specific rights to control and access your data. For more information on these rights and how to exercise them, visit corporate.harlequin.com/california-privacy.

LIS21R2

SPECIAL EXCERPT FROM

LOVE INSPIRED SUSPENSE
INSPIRATIONAL ROMANCE

*Out horseback riding, Dr. Katherine Gilroy
accidentally stumbles into a deadly shoot-out and
comes to US marshal Dominic O'Ryan's aid. Now with
Dominic injured and under her care, she's determined to
help him find the fugitive who killed his partner...before
they both end up dead.*

Read on for a sneak preview of
Mountain Fugitive *by Lynette Eason,*
available October 2021 from Love Inspired Suspense.

Katherine placed a hand on his shoulder. "Don't move,"
she said.

He blinked and she caught a glimpse of sapphire-blue
eyes. He let out another groan.

"Just stay still and let me look at your head."

"I'm fine." He rolled to his side and he squinted up at
her. "Who're you?"

"I'm Dr. Katherine Gilroy, so I think I'm the better
judge of whether or not you're fine. You have a head
wound, which means possible concussion." She reached
for him. "What's your name?"

He pushed her hand away. "Dominic O'Ryan. A
branch caught me. Knocked me loopy for a few seconds,
but not out. We were running from the shooter." His eyes
sharpened. "He's still out there." His hand went to his
right hip, gripping the empty holster next to the badge

on his belt. A star within a circle. "Where's my gun? Where's Carl? My partner, Carl Manning. We need to get out of here."

"I'm sorry," Katherine said, her voice soft. "He didn't make it."

He froze. Then horror sent his eyes wide—and searching. They found the man behind her and Dominic shuddered.

After a few seconds, he let out a low cry, then sucked in another deep breath and composed his features. The intense moment lasted only a few seconds, but Katherine knew he was compartmentalizing, stuffing his emotions into a place he could hold them and deal with them later.

She knew because she'd often done the same thing. Still did on occasion.

In spite of that, his grief was palpable, and Katherine's heart thudded with sympathy for him. She moved back to give him some privacy, her eyes sweeping the hills around them once more. Again, she saw nothing, but the hairs on the back of her neck were standing straight up. "I think we need to find some better cover."

As if to prove her point, another crack sounded. Katherine grabbed the first-aid kit with one hand and pulled Dominic to his feet with the other. "Run!"

Don't miss
Mountain Fugitive *by Lynette Eason,*
available October 2021 wherever
Love Inspired Suspense books and ebooks are sold.

LoveInspired.com